IO670442

Yellow
Blue Bus
Means
I Love
You

MORSE HAMILTON

Yellow Blue Bus Means I Love You

GREENWILLOW BOOKS
New York

The quotation on page vii is from *Doctor Zhivago* by Boris Pasternak, translated by Max Hayward and Manya Harari, published by Pantheon Books, © 1958 in the English translation Wm. Collins Sons & Co., Ltd., London.

The quotation on page 137 is from "Choirboys and Starlings" by Charles W. Pratt, copyright 1985 by Charles W. Pratt, from *In the Orchard* by Charles W. Pratt, published by The Tidal Press in 1986. Reprinted by permission of the author.

Copyright © 1994 by Morse Hamilton. All rights reserved. No part of this book may be reproduced or utilized in any form or by any means, electronic or mechanical, including photocopying, recording, or by any information storage and retrieval system, without permission in writing from the Publisher, Greenwillow Books, a division of William Morrow & Company, Inc., 1350 Avenue of the Americas, New York, NY 10019.
Printed in the United States of America
First Edition
10 9 8 7 6 5 4 3 2 1

Library of Congress
Cataloging-in-Publication Data
Hamilton, Morse.
Yellow blue bus means I love you /
by Morse Hamilton.
p.   cm.
Summary: Fifteen-year-old Tim, a Russian-born boy finding a new life in America, is not sure he likes his exclusive boarding school until he meets the lovely Phoebe and experiences both love and sex.
ISBN 0-688-12800-9
[1. Boarding schools—Fiction.
2. Schools—Fiction. 3. Russian Americans—Fiction.] I. Title
PZ7.H18265Ye   1994
[Fic]—dc20
93-19408   CIP   AC

■

FOR
MIRIAM LANSKOY,
ALEX GABAY,
MARINA GASSEL,
SERGY CHEBATAROV,
AND
EUGENE SIGALOVSKY

■

■

I'll stay with you a little,
my unforgettable delight,
for as long as my arms
and my hands and my lips
remember you.
I'll put my grief for you
in a work that will endure
and be worthy of you.

BORIS PASTERNAK

■

CoNtents

WiNter

It was dark out. Timur Borisovich Vorobyov—it's too hard for Americans to pronounce, so let's just say Tim—was slip-sliding through the snow, trying to make it back to campus before they closed the doors to the dining hall. He was hungry—he was born hungry, but that's another story. His father, who thinks he's a funny guy, says he probably has one of those worms in his stomach (in Russian you say *solityor*).

Not.

That day Tim was practically starving because he hardly ever made it to breakfast and he'd already skipped lunch to go to the gym office to get a sports excuse so he wouldn't have to run the Daily Mile in a snowstorm, which they make you do up there even if you're hacking your lungs out. If Homer the Greek, the blind poet who wrote *The Odyssey*, had gone to this school, they would probably have told him, C'mon, big guy, no excuses, hustle them buns.

As soon as his last class was over—at 6:15, because at Aviary Prep they have two hours of classes *after* sports— Tim had run through practically a blizzard to get a box of throat lozenges from Cormorant's Drugstore on Front Street. His throat killed. He knew from experience that if he went to the infirmary all they'd do was give him an envelope containing six white pills that practically knock you out, so you aren't physically able to keep your eyes open in Ms. Snipe-Dowitcher's English class.

Snipe-Do was all right—for an English teacher—it's just that Tim was much better at math and science where you didn't have to spill your guts all the time or tell your secret beliefs to people you hardly knew. Around other people,

Tim maintained a calm and cool exterior, but inside it was just the opposite.

His shitty Timex watch had stopped again, but he knew it had to be at least 6:39, and at 6:45 sharp they closed the doors to the dining hall. If you were, like, two seconds late, the obese Mr. Smew was there, on the inside, holding his digital watch in front of his fat, ugly nose and shaking his bowling-ball head. All Tim had had to eat that whole day was the box of shlurpy cherry-flavored throat lozenges his mouth was full of. He knows, by the way, that you aren't supposed to put them in your mouth all at once, but you don't know how hungry he was. Or how bad his throat hurt.

He remembers all this as though it happened yesterday, and not over a year ago. He was fifteen at the time and "emotionally reticent—he seems young for his age," as one of his teachers (Snipe-Do) said in her report home. Don't worry so much, Boris (his father) said. Would you rather be old for your age?

The town plow had been there ahead of him and made a roadway between steep banks of snow. From the lowering sky more snow was coming down in big, soft flakes that landed on your hot upturned face. The plow's engine was still grinding away somewhere on the other side of the hill. *Her* big throat never got sore. You could see her flashing lights swooping through the bare trees and on the sides of the white wooden houses, where most teachers and a few lucky girls got to live.

The smell of somebody's supper wafted on the evening air.

He stopped for a second at the top of Branch Lane to catch his breath and try to snap the snap on his brown jacket, which had fit fine the summer before when he was trying it on with his mom at Macy's, only now it was trying to strangle him. Also, his hands and wrists were freezing because nobody knew what had happened to his gloves (though suspicions fell on his roommate, one Freddy Goatsucker, about whom more later).

It was like in that poem, "Stopping by Woods on a Snowy Evening," by the great American poet, Robert Frost. Tim loves this poem, probably because none of his English teachers ever tried to explain it to him. If they did, he wouldn't be able to stand it, probably.

He was standing there, with blocks to go before he ate, literally burning up with fever. The next morning they took his temperature, and it was 104 degrees Fahrenheit, or 40 degrees Centigrade. The school doctor said he had psittacosis, which is like pneumonia, only worse. The nice nurse, the one who said, "Call me Ellie," stated that in the old days before antibiotics, Tim's time probably would have been up. Then they would have had to get out the plow again and dig a hole in the frozen ground so they could stick what was left of poor Timur next to Daniel Webster or one of the other local heroes.

Then nobody would act like he was a wimp for saying he felt too sick to go to swim practice, since swimming was one of the few subjects Tim Boyd liked.

He was standing there in the semidark, trying to catch his breath and snap his snap, when in the house he just happened to be standing next to (fate?) somebody turned on their light. He looked, and Phoebe Sayornis, this girl who was in two of his classes—he didn't know her very well, though—walked over to the window to get something. And she must have just gotten out of the shower or something, because she didn't have any clothes on.

When he breathed, which he had to after a while, it looked like he was smoking cigarettes.

I know what you're thinking: that Tim went there on purpose to peep in her window, but he didn't, I swear to God. He was just walking by—it's a shortcut all the kids take. When the light went on he did what any normal guy would do: look up. Besides, seeing someone naked isn't that big a deal for Tim Boyd, who lived for four years in New York City, the smut capital of the world.

Snow was falling through his open mouth, down his hot, raging throat. It got under his collar and started piling up on his sweaty head, since guys in this country don't think it's cool to wear warm fur hats.

She wasn't doing anything special, just walking back and forth, calmly picking out her clothes for tomorrow or whatever. Her lips were moving, but outside you couldn't hear anything, except for the falling snow, which, if you've ever listened to it, sounds like fingers touching fingers. He kept expecting somebody else to loom up behind her, but the rest of the house stayed dark. The only other lights were the lights they always leave on downstairs in the front hall. The other girls were probably at the dining hall, happily eating mystery meat, mashed potatoes and brown gravy, and dark, rich chocolate pudding. They allow seconds, even thirds.

She was probably just singing one of her favorite songs.

Other people had girlfriends. He wondered if he ever would.

She came over to the window and cupped her hands to the glass, looking like a big fish in an aquarium. Like a pink mermaid. Tim lifted his frozen arms slightly from his sides, but if she saw him she probably just thought he was a snowman some fac brats had built. Pretty soon she turned away, and all he could see was her shoulders, slightly curved.

You know how young kids don't realize that when it's

dark out you can't see *out*, but other people can see *in*? Well, it's probably a chauvinist thing to say, but he wanted to protect her. He felt like writing an anonymous note, telling her to please pull her shade. *People are seeing in! Signed, A Friend.*

But he didn't.

If one of his teachers had come along and said, Tim, is that you, son? What on earth are you doing out here? he would have simply pointed and let them kick him out for peeping, if that's one of the many things they kick you out for.

But nobody else came along.

After a while the light went out. He waited for several seconds, but the window just looked like a regular window where there isn't anybody home. So he started running, his boots slipping out from under him, the cold air stinging his bare hands. He ran with all his might up and over the hill, all the way to the dining hall, trying to get there before they closed the doors.

■

The name of the school isn't really Aviary Prep, but it should be because of all the Pewits and Peckerwoods that go there (old family names). Boris says if you're going to tell the truth about people in this country, you have to change their names first. Otherwise they can sue the pants off you. So Tim got all the names out of the bird book his dad keeps in the bathroom, in case anyone in their family ever decides to take up birding. It's called *A Field Guide to the Birds*, by Roger Tory Peterson (Eastern Edition). The idea came to him one day when he was just sitting there, turning the pages, and discovered everyone he knew was in there, whether friend or foe.

* * *

It wasn't Tim's idea to go to Aviary Prep in the first place. You have to understand this in order to understand everything else that happened. In Russia they don't have this barbaric custom of sending their kids away to boarding school at the tender age of fifteen. In Russia, even when you go to university, you usually live at home. Tim didn't understand why he couldn't just go to the neighborhood high school like all his New York friends, but if you want to know the truth his parents were obsessed with education.

On the way up to New Hampshire—it took about five hours—they kept laying this guilt trip on him, making it seem like they had left Russia and everything they knew behind and come to this faraway country just so he could go to this prestigious boarding school. That that's why his mom had spent the last four years slaving away at two jobs and why his dad taught four sections of Russian Conversation at Columbia, even though his specialty was Russian literature.

It was for his own good, they kept saying from the front seat. Someday he would thank them.

His parents had lived in the United States for just over four years, their English was goddamn terrible, but they were convinced they knew everything there was to know about this country. Whereas all they really knew was what other Russians, friends and relatives who had arrived first and helped them to immigrate, told them. And Tim knew that a lot of that was just prejudice and misunderstanding, like that "Boyd"—which is what they had their name legally changed to—was the best translation of "Vorobyov."

Not.

"Vorobyov" comes from "sparrow." Once upon a time, in another time and place, this was a very distinguished

name—Tim's great-grandfather was a famous biologist. But
after the Revolution their family, like many others, had to
downplay their ancestry. They had to say that a few members of the educated classes may have sneaked in, but most
of their forebears were factory workers, good proletarians.

It wasn't easy to reason with his parents when they
started acting like adults.

American public schools were a waste of time, his mom
said. They were like American television, catering to the
lowest common denominator. Fortunately there were excellent private schools, among which Aviary Prep was one of
the best. Free Enterprise meant that you got to decide how
you spent your money. Since Timka was a smart boy, getting a good education was naturally the number one prior-
ity, even if it cost—here she lapsed into English—*beek
bucks* (big bucks).

"Sixteen *beek* ones a year," said his father in the rearview
mirror. "*Slava bogu*, you got the partial scholarship."

Aviary Prep was where senators and judges sent their
kids, even Democrats who *said* they were in favor of public
education. Maybe one day Timur would become a senator
or Supreme Court justice. Maybe even President.

Not unless a two-thirds majority of both houses of Congress voted to amend the Constitution, Tim was thinking
in the back seat. And then it would have to be ratified by
the legislatures of three-fourths of the states.

But he kept his thoughts to himself. It was his mother's
fantasy, not his.

At all times Timur carried a mental map of the former
Soviet Union in his head. They had reached roughly the
same latitude as Yalta, in Crimea, a place that had personal
significance for him. For many generations, before Stalin,
Tatari—here you say Tartars—lived peaceably in Crimea.

Like many Russians, Tim's mother had *Tatar* blood in her—since how far back, nobody knew. You could see this in her round face and Asian features. He personally looked more Russian, like his dad—tall and blond—but he peered out at the world through Tartar eyes.

Under Stalin the Crimean Tartars were herded into box-cars and transported to Central Asia, so they couldn't cause any problems to the State. Since these facts came to light, Timur had felt a solidarity with the Crimean Tartars, who naturally wished to return to their homeland on that lovely peninsula which extends into the Black Sea. He vacationed in Crimea once with his family. There were cicadas humming in the cypress trees—not like Moscow or New England, where already in September you could smell the dying leaves.

They got off the interstate and drove down a state highway all crisscrossed with shadows, keeping an eye out for the house Boris was going to buy when he became a rich American writer like Vladimir Nabokov, author of *Lolita* and other sexy novels. This was a family joke. Tim's dad was also an author, but mainly of humorous articles, which appeared in *Novoye Russkoye Slovo*, the Russian émigré newspaper published in New York. Unlike Vladimir Vladimirovich, Boris had an ear only for Russian. But he didn't like to admit this and so found many pretty white houses with black shutters to purchase when the time came.

Much sooner than Tim wanted, a sign said WEBBER'S POND, NH, HOME OF THE AVIARY PREPARATORY SCHOOL SINCE 1801. And whereas before they had been cruising along, practically making his mom seasick going around some of the curves—"Borya, enough!"—they quickly slowed down to well within the speed limit—30 mph (or 50 km/h)—and Boris sat up straight, and they drove down the quietest streets Tim had ever seen out the back window of a car. There weren't any apartment buildings or nuclear power plants or other signs of civilization as we know it today, just houses older than the United States—which to Americans is *old*—shading themselves behind big leafy trees.

They were driving down Main Street, and he could have died, because instead of using the little map they send you after you mail in your first check, his dad pulled over to the curb and asked this kid who was just walking along in a jacket and tie—he probably thought they were scumbag tourists because who else would be driving a '79 Buick with only AM radio and New York plates?—if he could tell please where is the Rookery Dormitory for Boys. "Sure," said the kid, coming over to the curb and putting his hand on the roof of their car. He *looked* like a normal guy with zits and everything, but then he started giving these incredibly intelligent directions, calling Boris "sir," and that's when it finally dawned on Tim, who couldn't sink any lower in the backseat, that two T. Boyds had applied for admission and they let the wrong one in.

Then they were schlepping his stuff up three flights of stairs to the top floor of what was to be his home away from home, and there was a gang of strange boys who would probably never want to be friends with him playing hockey in the hall with somebody's sneaker. They stood still until they were sure it wasn't one of their teachers, coming to scold them—then the shoe went flying again.

Tim's room, when they finally succeeded in unlocking the door, had two metal beds, two chests of drawers, two desks with gooseneck lamps, and one metal wastebasket (already dented before Tim arrived). He was standing up his *American Heritage Dictionary* and atlas and a few other useful books between two blocks of petrified wood that his

Aunt Sonya had brought back from the Grand Canyon in the State of Arizona, when the door opened and a kid walked in. "Tim Boyd?" he said, holding out his hand. "Welcome to AP, Tim. I'm Bob White, senior proctor."

Tim mumbled "hi" and shook his hand.

"You folks aren't by any chance Connecticut Boyds, are you?" Bob White asked. "Just wondering—we've had a lot of Boyds here."

"No," his dad said, "Moscow Boyds. Boris," he said, also shaking the senior proctor's hand.

His mother stepped out of the closet, where she had been hanging up Tim's brand-new school clothes. She also shook Bob White's hand. "Yevnicia," she said, "Or just Yeva"— she was smiling so hard all her new dental work was showing—"easier."

"Ah," said Bob, taking a step backward. "You're my Russians. I thought it would be Pijewski. See, there's a Pijewski on my list. From Boston."

Boris had a look over his shoulder. "Pronounced 'Piyeffski'—it's Polish name. Like the poet."

"You don't say," said Bob. Then, suddenly, smiling, "Well, welcome to AP *and* America. There are probably a lot of things you'll have to get used to. I have to stay here and greet the other new boys, but feel free to roam around, tour the campus. If you have any questions I can answer, just holler."

His dad had a big smile on his face, so Tim was thinking, Oh, shit, he's going to make a joke. But Bob White's last speech went by too fast for Boris. He looked at Tim, who quickly held up his hand: Bye. So Boris held up his hand, too. He said, "See you late-or, Ollie Gate-or."

"Such nice young man," his mom said when Bob White

had left. She crossed her arms over her chest and stood on her tiptoes. "Like Kennedy, almost," she said in a soft voice.

She meant that Bob White looked rich, had nice clothes and straight teeth.

Boris put his big elbow in Timur's side and mentioned that, frankly speaking, if he was Timka he would want to be friends with a nice guy like Bob.

Tim went back to arranging his books. He knew that he was kind of shy, by American standards, but some guys here weren't shy enough. Also, why was Bob White smiling so much? Over here everybody was always smiling. If you don't believe it, look around next time you're driving down the street. In Russia only crazy people smiled all the time.

But that's only half the truth. He was also wishing he could take back the clothes his dad had talked him into buying at Buzzard's Men's Store on Seventh Avenue, where Cousin Vadim worked, and buy all new stuff out of cool catalogs. He imagined wearing a blue sweater, the color of the sky, and going up to people and sticking out his hand. Hi, my name's Tim Boyd. If you have any questions, just holler.

The truth is that from day one, part of him fell in love with Aviary Prep and everything it stood for. After what happened, it's not easy to admit this, but what's the point of writing your memoirs if you're not going to tell the truth?

Also, he was used to his parents because he had known them all his life, but now he looked and his father was wearing a cowboy shirt like his hero, Ronald Reagan. But unlike Reagan, he never rode horseback or stayed on his diets, so his stomach bulged around his big nickel-plated belt buckle. His mother was pudgy, too, not like American moms. Also, why did she have to dye her hair so red?

It's probably not a very nice thing to say, but he started wishing that they would hurry up and leave—if they weren't going to take him home with them, which was still his number one choice. But first they had to go back outside and tour the campus, speaking Russian in unnecessarily loud voices, as if to advertise that they were foreigners. Tim kept answering in English. It was getting to be their habitual way of talking to each other. He noticed, by the way, that only his dad drove an American car. Other kids were arriving in Volvos and Hondas and BMWs.

Finally, after slowly walking around all the buildings so that Boris and Yeva could ooh and aah and say how much AP resembled their idea of a small college, they ended up back in the parking lot of the Rookery Dormitory for Boys. Incidentally, it was one of the oldest buildings on campus. Over the main entrance were chiseled the immortal words of William Blake, the school's motto: NO BIRD SOARS TOO HIGH, IF HE SOARS WITH HIS OWN WINGS.

Yeva's eyes brimmed with tears. She stood on her toes and held Timur for like a whole minute (Mama, please!). His father waited shyly by the lilac bushes. When it was his turn, he solemnly kissed him on both cheeks and then on the crown of his head. Then he quickly opened the door on the passenger side—the other door was welded shut—and scooted over so that Yeva could climb in after him. She had to slam the heavy door twice to get it to stay shut. Their heads were hanging out both sides as the big car backed around and drove out the driveway. They continued to flap their arms until the car disappeared over the top of the hill.

■

He didn't feel like going back to his room, so he followed a well-worn path leading away from preppy clothes and smiles and signs saying SINCE 1801, past some tennis courts, out to the playing fields. A concrete bridge arched over the Little Skua River. A girl was leaning over one side. He kept on going, across more playing fields, into the woods beyond. The school grounds seemed to go on forever (it was a natural illusion). He walked for perhaps an hour, but finally came out of the woods, onto a different highway from the one they had taken. There was a Sunoco station on a hill, and beyond it a motel-restaurant. A little sign like a shield said TO INTERSTATE. Unfortunately, there was no McDonald's where you could buy a couple of Big Macs and a thick chocolate shake.

He walked along the highway until he came to a second path that led back into the woods. What would Bob White think, he was wondering, if he ever saw any of the places Tim had lived: the tiny apartment in Moscow, where he had spent the first ten and a half years of his life—two rooms, a minuscule kitchen, and a bathroom the size of a closet; or the apartment in Queens they shared with the Truskinovskys when they first came to this country—it had seemed so big when they first arrived; or the even bigger one they lived in now, near Columbia University. They had never owned any new furniture. Their couch sagged. The leather on his dad's chair had long ago split in the seat. The only ornaments were books—shelves of books, stacks of books, boxes of books. Also, a few black-and-white photographs, mostly of relatives or his parents' favorite authors.

It wasn't that he was ashamed to have lived in these places—they were *his* places, his personal landscape. But he couldn't imagine taking someone like Bob White home with him. More than ever, he felt like he was living a double life.

He wandered in the woods for some time—he was going

in the right direction, but in a roundabout way. After a while it got almost too dark to see. There were bells ringing in the distance. When at last he emerged onto the playing fields, the lights were already on in all the school buildings, people's shadows flitted by like bats, and the doors to the dining hall were locked tight. The kitchen staff was already mopping up.

He climbed the stairs in the Rookery Dorm for Boys. The door to his room was wide open. Inside, his new roommate, Freddy Goatsucker, was Scotch-taping pictures of naked women on all the walls. Freddy's father was vice president of a big oil company in Alaska. They lived in California, though. He asked Tim what his SSAT scores were. "You're only here because you're smart," the Goatsucker said. He said he wasn't bragging or anything but he had two Rolexes and showed them to Tim. He said Tim's watch (a Timex) was—"no offense"—a piece of shit.

■

More bells started bonging. Out in the hallway, kids trooped by. "Check-in time," said Freddy. He had gone to AP as a ninth grader, so Tim followed him.

It's hard to explain to someone who has never gone to boarding school in America, but at the end of the hallway there was just an ordinary-looking door. Usually it was locked and you had to stand there knocking until someone decided they heard you, but tonight it was open wide. You went inside and you were in an elegant apartment with carpets and sofas and paintings on the walls. It was your dorm parents' apartment, where you were supposed to go if you ever had a problem or just wanted to talk to a grown-up.

They had cider and cookies, then they went around the

room and everybody introduced themselves, except when it got to Tim's turn, Dr. Whimbrel, who spoke at least five foreign languages, said, *"Zdrastvooitye, Timofey, kak vy pozhivaete?"*

Everybody was staring at him.

"Timothy is from Moscow by way of New York," Dr. Whimbrel explained. "How do you like America, Tim?" he said, carefully enunciating each word, like he was talking to the village idiot. *"Kak vam nravitsa nasha strana?"*

"It's okay," Tim said. "My name's Timur, not Timofey. I was named after a character in a Russian children's book, *Timur i evo kommanda,* by Arkady Gaidar. It was my parents' favorite when they were growing up."

He was used to being singled out like this—it had happened every semester in New York, too. Still, he could feel the blood rush to his cheeks. It took about five seconds before his vision cleared and he was able to concentrate on what other guys were saying.

He wondered if it would be all right to stand up and take another cookie, since his stomach kept making rude noises.

Doc said to call him Doc. He did most of the talking. He didn't seem that funny to Tim, but all the seniors, who got dibs on the sofas, where they were practially sitting in each other's laps, kept hooting, so maybe it was dry wit. After he had been there for a couple of semesters, Tim would probably think Doc was a riot. As it was, he laughed when everyone else did.

Doc was their dorm father.

Their dorm mother—"Ms., if you don't mind," Whimbrel—was kind of hot-looking to be married to Doc, who had only a few gray hairs combed carefully over his otherwise bald head. Not that it was any of his business. Ms. Whimbrel was Assistant Director of Admissions and taught

Sex and Human Values. She also sat on the Disciplinary Committee.

Her son by a different marriage was one of the seniors. When he introduced himself in a barely audible voice, all the older guys went, "Ker-iss, Ker-iss!" Chris—that was his name: Chris Kite—raised his clasped hands first on one side and then the other. He had long hair in front of his face like a curtain, which every once in a while he jerked back.

"Must be nice to be a star," said his mom, looking at him with a big smile. You could tell she liked him. To Tim he looked like a *fartsovchik*—i.e., one of those creepy black marketeers who come up to you on Tverskaya Street and whisper, "You want hashish? You want girls?"

The rest of the time they just talked about what the rules were, but at least Bob White put the plate of cookies in the middle of the floor—they were gone in less than two seconds. (Luckily Tim has good reflexes.)

You couldn't build bonfires or make love to girl students in your room, or smoke dope or drink alcohol anywhere.

"If you have to smoke tobacco—"

"Even though it's bad for you," Ms. Whimbrel said.

"—do it in the Butt Room, not your room," said Doc. "If you aren't sure what the rules are, you'll know when you break one," he added ironically.

When the meeting was over, Tim went up to this one kid who had said he was from Manhattan, too, but it turned out he lived on Park Avenue and they couldn't think of that much to say to each other. Somebody mentioned something about popcorn, but nobody ever popped any, so after a while Tim just went back to his room.

When he got there, the lights were off and six kids, including Chris Kite, were standing by the window, looking through binoculars.

"Hey, shut the door," somebody said.

He stood behind them. With his naked eye all he could see was another dorm, more or less identical to the Rookery, on the other side of the quad. Practically all the windows were lit up—like so many color TVs piled up on top of each other. For at least a minute nobody went peep, all you could hear was six guys breathing, then somebody whispered, "Oh, my god, she's taking her shirt off."

"Where, where?"

"Top floor, one two three fourth from the right. Look, she's pushing them up. What's she trying to do, make them stick out more?"

"I'll do that for you, honey."

"I won't use my hands."

They were "birding," one of the more popular sports at AP.

Freddy let him look through his binoculars, but he wasn't quick enough to see anything that exciting. By the time he found the right window and got both lenses in focus, they had either pulled the shade or turned the lights off. The windows he could see into just had girls sitting around, talking.

He wondered what were they talking about.

He felt a little funny, spying on other people without their knowledge or permission, but he didn't want to act like a geek or worse the first night, so he just sat on his bed and waited. But after a while he said calmly, "You guys, I want to sleep."

Chris looked at him like he was going to spit, but somebody knocked on the door and called, "Bed check"—and the room quickly emptied out.

"We should charge ten bucks an hour," Freddy said later, in the dark, when Tim thought he was the only one still awake. "We'd make a fortune."

■

The next morning, after breakfast, there were orientation exercises down by the river. The whole school was there— so many kids it dazzled your eyes. Only new kids (like Tim) wore Aviary Prep T-shirts, though.

You had to do seven different trust exercises, like fall off the side of the humpbacked bridge into your classmates' open arms or crawl around an obstacle course blindfolded, holding on to the cold hand of the stranger in front of you and the warm hand of the stranger behind. Only the leader could see where you were going. It was like on "Sesame Street," where you learned to cooperate, but it also taught conformity.

But nobody likes a cynic.

He kept looking for someone he recognized. He was beginning to wonder if his dorm was supposed to be somewhere else. Then he saw his dorm brother, Chris Kite, and made the mistake of going up to him and saying, "Hey, Chris."

Chris looked at him, but didn't say anything. He had his arm draped over the shoulder of a girl whose shirt said PARTY NAKED. He put his hand on her breast and started rubbing it up and down. She looked startled, then smiled up at him.

Tim stood maybe twenty feet away, pretending he knew what everybody was waiting for.

After a while Freddy showed up with a freckle-faced girl who said, "Hi, you want to be our partner?"

"S-sure," he said, surprised he was visible to other members of the human race.

"This is Julie," Freddy said.

"Julie Crake," she said, shaking hands.

"Tim Boyd."

She had more red hair than he had ever seen on a human head, but she was a little on the plump side. "I don't speak Russian," she said. *"¿Habla usted Español?"*

"He speaks perfect English," Freddy said. "Better than us."

"No, it's not true. I make a lot of mistakes, especially articles and prepositions."

"God," said Julie. "I see what you mean." In her hand she had two cowboy bandannas. "Here," she said, and tied one around Freddy's eyes and then the other around Tim's. "Can you see?"

"Nope," said Freddy.

"Nope," said Tim.

"Good."

Her damp hands led them down to the river's edge, where they had to take turns getting into a wobbly canoe. According to the written instructions that Julie read to them, this exercise was supposed to be a metaphor for the human condition:

> "We are all in the same boat. Christian, Muslim, Jew, atheist; black, yellow, brown, white; rich, poor. Only by pulling together can the family of nations all make it to the other shore."

Her voice came from the middle of the boat. You could feel the boat rock every time she moved.

"Start paddling," she said, telling them which side to put their oars on. She was their eyes, metaphorically speaking.

"Help, I'm getting drenched" she shouted. "Other side, other side!" They were all laughing. "Left, left—how do you say left in Russian?"

"Nalevo."

"Now lever? I can't say it. *Izquierdo, izquierdo.*" When they reached the middle of the river, the current was carrying them downstream. He had never been in a canoe in his life, much less paddled one, but he had earned his Junior Lifesaving Certificate at the Uptown Branch of the YMCA. He knew what to do in case they capsized.

Before that became necessary, however, the bow of the boat bumped against the other bank. Julie had been laughing too hard to warn them. Freddy clambered out first. "We set a new world's record," his voice said gleefully—but later it turned out their boat was the second slowest.

Julie had to shout at him, "Hold the boat, klutz! We're moving away." Finally Tim crawled over the thwarts and onto terra firma.

"Ah, Tim, you can take your blindfold off now."

When he pulled it up over his eyes, she was smiling at him like she liked him. He still felt like an alien from another planet, but at least he had somebody to stand next to and cheer the other boats with. Actually it was pretty fun.

Julie began telling him all her theories, like that if people would eat only vegetables there wouldn't be so much disease and war in the world. Tim didn't say anything one way or the other. Her face was covered with freckles, even her ears and the edges of her nostrils.

■

School at AP was different from the Booker T. Washington Junior High School on Columbus Avenue in Manhattan, where Tim had done his eighth and ninth grades. It was more like a Russian school—hard. Mostly he just tried to survive and get to all his classes on time. He had so much homework to do that he didn't get to bed till one or two in the morning. Then he had to get up at seven.

He liked biology and advanced algebra best. In history one kid would say something and it would make sense, then somebody else would say the complete opposite, and that would make sense, too, so he decided that even if Congress changed the Constitution he didn't want to be President.

He was hoping he could just take Russian and be the star of the class, but his parents said he had to take French because it was quote unquote the language of all educated people. It wouldn't have been so bad if he could have just said the words the way they looked on the page, without having to do funny things with his mouth that frankly speaking didn't feel a hundred percent masculine. He found he already knew some of the words—*journal, trottoir, restaurant*, etc.—because in the eighteenth and nineteeth centuries French had infiltrated Russian. Madame Oiseau seemed pretty impressed, so he told her a story his dad had told him, about the one Russian word that went the other way, became French—namely, *bistro*. When the Russian soldiers chased Napoleon back to Paris, they would go into small wine shops and ask for a drink—quickly, quickly, gesturing with their fingers. The Russian word for quickly—*bistro*—became the name for such establishments. Madame Oiseau listened to him, but she only smiled and shook her head. "I donut sink so," she said.

The kids who had taken French in their old schools, but flunked the placement exam, knew all the bad words, like *merde, pet de poule, couchez avec moi*. They kept asking Madame how to say seal in French, because the word is *phoque* and if you pronounce it right it sounds like the

F-word in English. Everyone always cracked up. Madame Oiseau would go, "Boot I donut see watt tease so fun knee. *Phoque, phoque.* This school is a zoo, yes?"

She even looked a little like a *phoque* in the black leather miniskirt she always wore.

After French came lunch, his favorite (smile). Everybody always said the dining hall food tasted like garbage, but in his school cafeteria in Moscow, under the giant portrait of Lenin, all you got was hard bread, kielbasa—mostly fat with a few microscopic pieces of meat—stale cheese, if you were lucky a pickle, maybe some potatoes or rice. In the fall there were sometimes wormy apples. As Albert Einstein, Tim's hero, would say, everything is relative.

■

After lunch came sports, then two more classes, then dinner. After dinner they were supposed to sit in their rooms reading, but half the guys in the Rookery were down in the Butt Room, smoking cigarettes and discussing God and girls, the two unresolved questions of the universe. Chris Kite was the authority on chicks because, according to legend, he had been caught humping the principal's daughter in the recreation room of Aerie House. For punishment he was put on probation, which meant he had to check in early on weeknights. If he was caught breaking any more rules, it would be good-bye, Chris.

Everyone was in awe of him, though according to Freddy, Karen Dunlin was a nympho who would let anybody have sex with her, including the men who worked in the dish room. Her parents had withdrawn her from the school before her case could come before the Disciplinary Committee. They put her in a boarding school in Massachusetts that specialized in troubled children, but as soon as they drove away, she jumped out her window. Luckily her dorm only had two floors and she landed in some bushes. Now she was in a "home"—i.e., not a real home.

He wondered how anybody could hate their parents so much that they would do something like that. Mr. and Mrs. Dunlin seemed like nice people. Mr. Dunlin always said "Hi there!" when he passed Tim on the quad.

The Karen business was supposed to be a big secret because if prospective parents found out that the principal's daughter was suicidal, they might have second thoughts about sending their children there.

Chris claimed to know the secret of how to get into any girl's pants. Psychology. It was the subject he was planning to specialize in in college. "You have to realize that they want it as much as you do. Once you understand that, the rest is easy. They all claim they want a nice, sweet, liberated boy—that's bullshit. Really, they'd be embarrassed to let a guy like that even touch them. If you look gross on the outside but act sensitive underneath, they'll be coming up to you and asking you to break them in."

"Oh, yeah?" said Freddy, taking a quick drag off his cigarette. "I tried that shit with Julie Crake, but she told me to grow up. She's probably a lesbo, huh?"

Everybody looked at Chris who, after glancing at the door, took a sandwich bag full of herbs and spices from his back pocket. "When all else fails . . . ," he said, opening up the Ziploc seal and putting his nose inside. "Nicaragua gold, the greatest aphrodisiac known to man."

■

Every once in a while, when no one was expecting it, Tim made an obscene or sarcastic remark. Like, one time he blurted, "What's the Russian word for syphilis?" (The answer is *Rotchyercockoff*. Someone had had to explain this joke to him at his old school.) At first there was a stunned silence, then everyone cracked up. After a while he got the reputation for being a cynic—it meant nobody thought he was a geek or worse.

Deep down, though, he believed—or, rather, used to believe—that maybe geeks know something the rest of us don't. He even defended this one kid on the second floor who never came down to the Butt Room—he never left his room except to go to classes. Freddy claimed he peed in an empty Fluff jar that he kept under his bed—the Goat said he saw him emptying it once. The kid's name was David Crane, only everybody called him Ichabod.

Ick *was* a little strange, but he was pretty smart. He was the only tenth grader, besides Tim, who made an A- on the first biology test. He had lived in boarding schools all his life. In the summer he was sent away to camp.

Ick had made up his own religion. Every morning he would clear his mind of all mundane thoughts. Then he would try to picture the vastness of the universe and all the frozen and lifeless planets spinning in space. Also the many burning stars, like our sun. Then he would spend a few minutes calculating the odds against the existence of a planet like ours, hospitable to life, with flowers and trees, etc. And then, as he contemplated our blue planet from the point of view, he once told Tim, of somebody living on the red one—hence, by the way, his other nickname: "the boy from Mars"—he calmly meditated on the enormous odds against a person ever being born at all, because of all the millions of sperms that end up in Kleenexes or condoms, not to mention the odds against anyone surviving all the childhood diseases to his or her present age.

Working logically from this point of view, Ichabod would have an epiphany about just how unlikely and infinitesimal man is—woman, too. How petty his squabbles were, in places like Northern Ireland or the former Soviet Union. Once he had thought this all out, he would finally get out of bed and go around all day, not loving his fellow person exactly, but having pity on him/her for being so heinous.

His religion kept him from getting into fights with other kids, even members of the hockey team who liked to wait for him to come out of the science building so that they could walk behind him and imitate his walk (sort of like Big Bird's on "Sesame Street"). It was probably a good thing that he was a pacifist, because he was maybe 1.8 meters tall and only weighed about 50 kilos—it means tall and skinny.

Tim became a member of Ichabod's religion for about twenty-four hours, following an initiation ceremony that he has mostly blotted from his memory—it consisted of sitting in Ick's room with the lights out for nearly an hour, listening to him breathe. But then somebody (probably Frederick G. Goatsucker III) urinated in Tim's shampoo bottle, so Tim used his Magic Markers to draw mustaches and peckers on Freddy's pinups, and after that they were put on restrictions for a week for trying to punch each other in the hallway.

Doc Whimbrel broke it up. "Back to your rooms, boys," he said to the crowd gathered in the hall. "Don't you have anything better to do, such as homework?" He was wearing those half glasses that you have to bow down to see over the tops of.

Ichabod came out of his room long enough to whisper that he, Tim, who was sitting on the floor with his back against the wall, trying to catch his breath, was "too full of blood." After that they drifted apart.

■

Sometimes Tim worried that even this brief association with the boy from Mars had rubbed off on him. One morning that he would rather forget there was a loud crashing noise in his room. Doc Whimbrel used his master key to open the door. Behind him were kids in pajamas, trying to see in.

Tim was sort of sitting in his wastebasket.

"Timofey," Doc said. *"Shto sluchilos'?* What happened, son?" He was wearing a silk bathrobe like an actor in an old movie.

Before Tim could explain, Freddy Goatsucker came out of the shower with his towel over his shoulder and his ugly red pecker sticking out so that you had to see it whether you wanted to or not. Not. "Oh, he's always doing stuff like that," he said. "He was reading this book where the hero jumps into his pants, and he was wondering if it was really possible."

It was true that Tim's pants were bunched up around one of his feet. He looked at Doc Whimbrel's face for even the faintest flicker of interest. "I just fell over," he lied.

Doc Whimbrel looked at him sadly, but all he said was, "Hurry up, boys. You don't want to be late for your eight o'clocks."

■

Tim hardly remembers Phoebe Sayornis from his first semester at AP. She was in two of his classes—Sex and Human Values, and English. Both of them met after lunch. She always sat with one arm over the back of the empty seat next to her, breathing loudly as if pissed or bored. He asked her once if he could borrow a pencil. She rummaged in her purse, but all she found was a leaky pen that wrote purple. "Sorry," she said, looking at him for nine-tenths of a second.

Then, in October, her father was the Bunting Fellow, which means they paid him a small fortune to visit the school and tell all the tenth graders they wrote drivel. Freddy went around for about a week saying, "If only I could fall in love with Phoebe Sayornis, then maybe her dad would publish my stories, and I would be rich and famous." Freddy was always writing short stories, though he never read anything unless he had to. His dream was to write the Great American Novel.

Phoebe's dad was the fiction editor of *Pelican* magazine. That didn't seem like such a big deal to Tim. Sure, he had thumbed through *Pelican* while sitting on the john—who hasn't?—but he didn't notice any fiction. The women in the pictures looked like they'd be more interested in someone older, who knew what he was doing.

Besides, at AP half the kids had famous parents (not Tim, though). Frankly speaking, you tended to forget about parents up there.

He happened to be in the parking lot when her dad pulled up in his black Mercedes, and he and his wife (not Phoebe's mother) got out. The famous editor started shaking hands with the little group of mostly teachers who were there to meet him. He had a loud laugh, and when he shook someone's hand he repeated their name out loud, like he really knew it, it had just slipped his memory.

In his three-piece suit Mr. Sayornis was kind of overdressed for a school where the boys had to wear a jacket and tie, but most just knotted it loosely around their necks and wore sneakers instead of shiny black shoes. Some of the guys, like Tim, wore baseball caps.

Phoebe was standing practically in the bushes. When her dad saw her, he said, "Hi, honey!" in a very jovial voice. You could tell she didn't know if she should shake his hand like everybody else or hug him and give him a peck on the cheek.

The lady in the mink stole said, "Phoebe!" and hugged her for him.

■

All the tenth-grade English classes that met after sports had to go to the Bunting Room so that Mr. Sayornis could tear their stories apart for them. If you didn't go AP you might not know that Indigo Bunting was a rich alumnus who left the school at least a million dollars on the condition that they build a room to house his world-class collection of bird trophies. Specimens ranging from the American bald eagle to a hummingbird no bigger than a bumblebee adorned the walls, all of them, over the years, slowly molting for the last time, getting harder and harder, gathering dust.

It didn't bother Tim so much, being in there, but then his ancestors had been nomads and hunters, and he himself was an incorrigible carnivore. But Julie looked like any second she was going to puke. To make her feel better, he leaned over and whispered, "They should have mounted Mr. Bunting on the wall, if he was so concerned about his immortality."

Phoebe's dad said to call him Goshawk. He sat on the table, where the Disciplinary Committee met to decide which kids to kick out and which to just put on probation, and lit a cigarette. You're not supposed to smoke on campus, except in officially designated areas, but the faculty just sat in the front row with smiles on their faces. But if one of the kids had tried it, they wouldn't have been smiling.

"Your teachers are paid to feed your egos," Goshawk said, blowing smoke rings. "No offense, but I earn my living in the real world. So as I understand it my job is to play bad cop and tell you the bitter truth."

For some reason everybody laughed, a little nervously, and then since nobody volunteered, Snipe-Do turned around and said, "Julie, why don't you read your story about the homeless?"

Julie turned bright red. "Do I have to?" she said. "It's not very good."

"Hell no, you don't have to!" thundered Goshawk, tapping his ash on the floor for Mr. Ravenscroft, the janitor, to clean up. "Not if it isn't very good. Seriously, if more writers were as honest as you, there would be less guano for people like me to have to wade through." He was smiling at Snipe-Do, who was all smiles back, even though earlier she had complained that *Pelican* magazine exploited women. Maybe she was hoping he would publish some of *her* guano, which she was always reading to their class. "Go ahead, kid," he said to Julie, "don't mind me." So she sat up, took a deep breath, and began to read, but after only two sentences, he said, "Crap. Next?"

Julie sat there for a couple of seconds, the smile fading on her orangish lips, then quickly stood up, going, "Excuse me, excuse me," as she made her way down the row. When she had squeezed past the last kid's knees, she fled up the aisle and out through the glass doors, which clattered behind her.

Even though he only liked her as a friend, Tim felt like running after her.

But Phoebe's dad did that to all the kids. "You're not going to learn to be writers in some high-school English class," he said, "I don't care how many thousands of dollars they charge your parents for tuition."

Tim hoped that he would be saved by the bell, but Snipe-Do said, "Tim Boyd? You like to write." And whereas before he had been sitting in the darkening room, just one of the crowd, now everybody's eyes were looking at him.

The sound of his own voice startled him. He said, "On the 25th of March there occurred in St. Petersburg a very unusual and strange event." He stopped, expecting Mr. Sayornis to say "Crap!" When he didn't, Tim said: "Ivan Yakovlevitch, who was living on Ascension Street (by the way, his surname has been lost, even from his sign, which showed a gentleman with lathered cheeks and, underneath, the words 'Blood also let'—"

"Enough, already!" Mr. Sayornis said, putting his hand to his head. "Jesus, that's the most awful goddamn guano I think I've ever heard."

"I didn't write it," Tim's voice said. "I'm translating from memory. It's by Gogol, Nikolai Vasilievich."

Everyone cracked up.

Usually our hero doesn't have that much to say in class, but other times he can't believe the words that come out of his mouth. He expected Mr. Sayornis to be angry, but he just smiled, showing his teeth. "No, I knew someone would pull this. What's it from?"

"*Nos*—it means nose." He illustrated by touching his own.

Everyone laughed again, even, he noticed, Julie, who had snuck back in the room and was sitting with a pile of paper toweling in her lap.

Mr. Sayornis held up his small hands. "But our friend here . . ." he said in a booming voice. "What's your name, son?"

"Tim. Tim Boyd."

"Mr. Boyd, the class clown, is just proving my point. Remind me: When did Gogol live?"

"From 1809 until 1852."

"You see? This, unless I'm mistaken, is the end of the twentieth century. Herr Gogol or however you say his name is fine if you have the time and patience. Most readers nowadays are in a hurry. They pick up a book because they're stuck on a plane, and basically if they don't read they'll have to talk to the bozo sitting next to them. You have at the outside about one paragraph to hook them— otherwise they're going to turn on their headset and blot out the world by listening to rap music. Am I right?"

There was a second's pause, then everyone started clapping—even, Tim noticed, Julie Crake. She probably didn't want him to think she was mad at him, since he was only saying this for their own good.

Some of what Mr. Sayornis said made sense. Like, afterward, Tim always tried to make the opening of whatever he was writing sound as exciting as he could. But it made him wonder that the only story their visitor liked was by Arthur Creeper, maybe because the first sentence had a decapitated body in it. "Promising," the editor said, thoughtfully. "You've piqued my curiosity. I would read on."

When it was Phoebe's turn, she said, "I would prefer not to." Tim turned to look at her. She was sitting with her face at a slight angle, the forward cheek bright pink. He didn't make her read because she was his daughter. "It's okay, sweetheart," he said. "You know what a tough bastard I can be, but at least I'm honest."

This took place on the 31st of October. Some fac brats dressed like owls and penguins were sitting in the birch trees, which seemed to get whiter as night decended. You could see them through the high windows.

■

One day in Sex and Human Values he had the idea of trying to make friends with the editor's daughter, who seemed to be even lonelier than he was.

Ms. Whimbrel was saying, "No wonder you kids are confused about sex. Society keeps sending you mixed messages." All the tenth graders had to take S&HV—it was the state law or something. He was interested in the subject per se, just not the way they talked about it in there. You couldn't say tits or pussy, you had to say mammary glands and vulva. Even in his native tongue, he didn't know such technical terms.

Ms. Whimbrel also liked to pass around pictures of people's private parts all covered with chancres and scabs before lunch.

For the next class they were supposed to go downtown and buy a condom. That way if they should ever need one, like in the heat of the moment, it wouldn't seem like such a big deal. Katie Kiskadee, who flunked the first quiz because she couldn't remember what lesbians do—"I forgot how to spell it," she claimed—started going, "Oh my god, oh my god."

"Now, Katie, cut it out!" Ms. Whimbrel said, because Katie, who had asthma, was starting to hyperventilate. "It's a very ordinary thing to do. They're on a rack. All you have to do is pick out the kind you want and go up and pay for it. Get a Reese's Peanut Butter Cup, and no one will think twice."

Ms. Whimbrel was also a fanatic about masturbation, always mentioning new ways to do it (like with your other hand). At first it made his hair sweat—to hear a grown-up talking about such a personal matter like it was no big deal—but after a while he got used to it. You got used to everything in that class.

He wondered what *her* love life could be like, since for her sex was there mainly to relieve tension, like taking a Tylenol or an Excedrin.

Her philosophy seemed to be: If you're going to do it, it's better to just pull your pecker and get it over with so you can get your homework in on time. But since, according to the statistics from the *Boston Globe* that they had to memorize, 25.6 percent of fifteen-year-old girls surveyed said they had gone "all the way" at least once, it was better to be prepared.

The phrase "all the way" made his mind wander.

Ms. Whimbrel held up various contraptions for preventing pregnancy, explaining the advantages and disadvantages of each, like the Tupperware lady who was the first person to greet them when they arrived in Queens. Tim usually sat there, pretending he knew this stuff already, but really he was surreptitiously looking around the room, trying to guess who the 25.6 percent were.

He felt cheated.

Mr. Grosbeak, the man teacher, had a mustache like Joseph Stalin, but really he was nothing like the dictator, who killed at least 20 million people. It was hard to believe a person so ugly could find anyone to have coition with, but at least he was sarcastic. Once he held out his arms and flapped his hands, saying, "I'm a little fallopian tube."

He also told them what a merkin was.

Ms. Whimbrel smiled with all her teeth showing, but you could tell she wasn't that amused. Sex wasn't a joking matter for her.

Whenever anybody said something funny, Tim quickly looked at Phoebe. Different people notice different things, like a person's eyes or their mammary glands. Tim tended to notice their mouth—was it a mouth he wanted to kiss or *au contraire*?

On the day they found out they had to buy a condom, Phoebe's lips were slightly open. She had two squarish front teeth, like a little kid's.

He wondered if she was a virgin.

After class they just happened to leave the room together. He could so easily have said, You want to be partners? because Ms. Whimbrel said they could work in pairs if they wanted to. Do it! a voice said. But he was such a despicable chicken that he just went home and borrowed one of his roommate's.

Freddy the Goatsucker had a whole collection of rubbers in the bottom drawer of his dresser. Some were black and some had little bumps on them like a Russian pickle. And one, which he sent away for from a catalog after signing a statement swearing that he was twenty-one or older, was supposed to glow in the dark. They found out afterward you had to hold it under a bright light for about twenty minutes first.

Coming, dear, just let me shine this light on it a little longer.

■

His parents had wonderful news to tell him when he went home for Thanksgiving break. "Wait until dinner," his mother said, drying her eyes with a towel. "So much excitement in one week. We didn't want to interrupt your studies."

"It's simply unbelievable," said his father, brandishing a hair brush before the hall mirror.

They ate the delicious Peking turkey at Ping Sing restaurant on Broadway. His parents loved this restaurant because they understood the Chinese waiters' English, and vice versa. On this occasion, only a few other patrons were present. Tim couldn't help thinking of Moscow, where only rich people and foreigners could afford such feasts. But his appetite was good notwithstanding. The tender white meat did not turn to ashes in his mouth.

"Now are you going to tell me?" he asked, looking from one to the other.

"Oh, Timka, guess what? We have won a lot of money. I'm afraid even to say how much." She looked around, then whispered, "One million dollars."

"One million dollars!"

"It was a contest," his father explained, slowly shaking his head.

"Now we can fly Grandpa and *Baboolia* to the USA. Get them the best medical treatment. Buy a new car—a Cadillac, even."

Tim's grandfather had lung cancer; his grandmother—Baboolia, they called her—had Alzheimer's. Tim pictured them both, staring sadly out the window of their old apartment in Moscow. His grandpa, who had been a colonel in the Red Army, was always coughing, telling stories to anyone who would listen about the good old days before Perestroika, when people could still buy food and vodka in the stores. Baboolia was not a good listener. She lived in a world of her own, where life was glum.

They both hated Gorbachev and Yeltsin's guts.

He couldn't take in the news. "Are you sure it's a million—a one followed by six zeros?"

His father reached inside his jacket and took out a thick envelope. It was addressed to "Brenda Skeet—or current occupant of Apt. 9B." Tim leafed through the printed pages until he came to a check that did indeed say ONE MILLION DOLLARS. However, the check was made out to YOUR NAME HERE. And all along the bottom were the words VOID, VOID, VOID, VOID, VOID. He turned it over to where it said, "A chance to win an extra $25,000 if you mail in your order before December 12."

"Um, you guys, I think—in fact, I know—this is an ad. An advertisement. Capitalist propaganda. See, it says here, 'Imagine how you will feel when you see your name on the enclosed check.' "

"Where?" his mother said, breathless. "Show me."

Tim's father sat back and lit a cigarette. "I knew it was unbelievable. I was saying so from the beginning."

"An advertisement?" said Yeva, turning the check this way and that. "Not a million dollars? A hundred maybe?"

For several minutes nothing more was said. It was as if each had awakened to find himself or herself in a half-empty Chinese restaurant on Broadway on a cold, dark afternoon in November. Tim noticed that the leaves of the plastic kumquat tree had dust on them. However, during dessert, Boris leaned forward, conspiratorially. "Timka," he said, winking. "I have another good news for you. Not ad; fact. They have offered me job. Full-time lectureship at Brant College on Staten Island."

In Moscow Boris had been a teacher of Russian language and literature at one of the best schools—High School 27 in the Kievsky District of Moscow—but in America his English wasn't good enough to teach these subjects. Also, not that many schools here offer Russian language and literature. Did you know that there are more English teachers in Russia than students of Russian in America? Or that of those students in America who learn a foreign language, fewer than one percent take Russian—can you believe it?

Timur said, "Dad, congratulations. I'm so proud of you."

"Yes," said his mother, brightening. "It means we're moving in the spring. To a house . . ." She let the word sink in. They had never lived in a house before. ". . . on this island. Boris will be teaching Russian Conversation full-time."

"I am a lecturer," Boris said modestly, with his spoon in his mouth.

"Timushka, wait until you see our house. Three stories plus a basement. Wood paneling in all rooms. Big yard in back with peach tree. It needs, of course, a few adjustments, but it's perfect."

"Such a country!" said Boris.

Out on the street a few flakes of snow were blowing in the freezing wind. Tim and his mom stood shivering while Boris ran into a small vegetable market on Broadway to buy more cigarettes. Where they were standing, between 110th and 111th Streets, they already had Christmas trees for sale. For a few seconds, breathing the cold smell of the fir trees, Tim could imagine he was back in Moscow, in the cemetery where Boris's parents were buried.

He imagined trying to describe a market like this one to friends and relatives he hadn't seen in over four years. Any time, day or night, you can go there and buy something. Milk, bread, candy bars, newspapers. Canned goods. Whatever your heart desires. His friends would say, give us the address so that if we should ever be so lucky as to visit the USA, we can go to this store.

Sure, no problem.

He had imagined such conversations all the time when he first came here, but four years is a long time. Looking back now was like looking through the wrong end of a pair of binoculars.

That night the snow turned to rain, which whipped against the building (global warming). Long after everyone else had gone to bed, he was still up, working on his *Odyssey* paper, trying to prove that the true author was Telemachus, Odysseus's son—i.e., not an old blind man. (If you read the epic with an open mind, you will see for yourself. The whole first part is definitely told from Telemachus's point of view.)

When he finally conked out, he dreamed that his bed was rocking back and forth. He got up and went to the window. All the buildings on Viktorenko Street in Moscow were bobbing up and down in the Black Sea. *"Dyedooshka! Baboolia!"* he called, running out into the empty hall and up the stairs. When he pushed open the door of the roof, little waves were spilling over the sides. The moon was shining. There was water all around.

It might not sound that scary now, but at the time he nearly peed his pajama bottoms.

■

The day Snipe-Do gave back their *Odyssey* papers, Tim slouched in his seat—that way, if she wished to read his aloud, he could sit up and act surprised. But when she stalked in, papers spilling from her briefcase, you could tell she was in a foul mood. The class grew still as she stood on her tiptoes and wrote the word PLAGIARISM on the board. Then she turned around and asked if anybody could explain what that meant. Immediately all the Pewits and Peckerwoods raised their hands—Me, me!—so Tim (as usual) tuned out. For at least ten minutes they had to discuss what a heinous crime plagiarism was, since you aren't stealing a person's money or material goods, but their words and ideas.

Which, incidentally, he agrees with.

Then she said, "Somebody in this class has plagiarized," and all the kids went "Oooh!" Everybody looked around to see if they could tell who had done such a filthy deed, only some were probably thinking, Shit, she caught me. Tim wondered what would make an otherwise honest person do such a thing.

She continued to obsess on the subject. Like, what grade was she supposed to give this paper? So he started sketching a map of Crimea on the front of his notebook. In her opinion, the most suitable punishment was to just give the paper an A, since that's what the real author deserved.

The scarlet letter, he thought at the time.

Then she was handing back papers, and the next thing he knew, he was holding his, and it didn't have any of her usual comments on it, which you could never read anyway because her handwriting was like bird tracks. Instead it just had a big red A on the back, like somebody had stabbed a knife in it. He quickly looked up at her—she was watching him, but quickly turned away.

Nothing he could say to her after class would convince her that he had actually written his paper. "It's not your English, which I know is remarkable. It's this mixture of precocious observations that no kid your age could make and utter naïveté. I think any teacher would think it was plagiarized."

Maybe she was paying him a compliment in disguise?

"I wrote it," he said, nodding once. "Honest," trying to look honest. He wondered if he should swear to God.

She snatched the paper from his hands. "Listen to this: 'Telemachus believes that fidelity must be the foundation for all civilization.' "

"That trust must be?"

"Yes, but what's that supposed to mean?" Suddenly she was gathering her books. "Think of all the goddesses Odysseus screws."

His mind went blank. It was as if he had never read this book, which, by the way, he loved.

Of all the people he didn't want to have standing by the bulletin board, pretending to read cartoons from *The New Yorker* that were turning yellow with age, but really listening to every word they said, was Phoebe Sayornis, who piped up, "I just had a question about my grade. I can wait."

She was wearing her green parka with the hood back and her dark, wild hair spilling out.

He had never stood this close to Snipe-Do before. In class she acted all jaunty, always cracking jokes, but now he realized she must be at least thirty. If he hadn't hated her so much for not believing him, he would have probably felt sorry for her, since, according to Freddy, she and her husband were getting a divorce, and they had two kids under five.

"Look," she said, "you and I both know that plagiarism is almost impossible to prove. I don't have time to go through every book in the library just to track down this crackpot theory. So let's say I'm giving you the benefit of the doubt. Congratulations, you got an A. You should be happy."

It was useless to explain that happy he was not.

"Tim," she called out, as he started to leave. "If you can really write this well, why is it we so seldom get the benefit of your wisdom in class? If you never talk, how are we supposed to know who you are? Or what's going on inside?"

She had him there. Sometimes he talked—if it was a question he was sure he knew the answer to. But usually he didn't trust his voice to say out loud in correct English what he was thinking. Maybe he was more of a writer than a speaker. Also, frankly speaking, it seemed like whatever he thought was the exact opposite of what everybody else was saying, so he would end up getting into an argument with Sarah Shrike, who always called people who didn't agree with her some kind of "ist" or "phobe." And Snipe-Do never said, "Now, Sarah, that's not a nice thing to say." She just laughed.

It's also probably not a nice thing to say, but sometimes he wondered if Snipe-Do could really be that smart, since, according to her, Homer was overrated (wrong). She didn't even want to teach him, she said, because of all the blood and guts in his work, but he was an official part of the curriculum, left over from when Aviary Prep was an all-boys' school.

Probably he should have written on one of the suggested topics. That's what Freddy, who was in Snipe-Do's morning class, did. He wrote on "How Homer's *Odyssey* Is Degrading to Women." And Ibrahim, the black kid from Detroit, discussed "Racism in the 'Cyclops' Episode." They both got B+.

But no, Tim wanted to be original.

Pride goeth before a fall.

Phoebe glanced at him as he passed. He felt like telling her that except for his *American Heritage Dictionary*, he hadn't used any outside sources. I made it all up myself— swear to God.

* * *

On the way back to the dorm, carrying his rolled-up paper in his hand, he could see the black outline of everything against the winter sky. He made sure the door to his room was locked, put his paper in his suitcase, which was under his bed, then went into the closet and pulled his pecker. But contrary to what his Sex and Human Values teacher told them, it didn't relieve his stress or make him feel any better. *Au contraire*, it seemed like now he didn't have anything to look forward to in life.

He woke up before dawn and couldn't go back to sleep. Nothing helped, not turning the pillow over or lying very still with both eyes closed, breathing slowly, in and out.

In his imagination he started building a raft like Odysseus and just sailing home, except that unlike the Aegean Sea the Atlantic Ocean is freezing cold. One big wave and he would probably perish from hypothermia. He could see his water-soaked body washing up on the New Hampshire coastline. Somebody would check all the books in the library and they wouldn't be able to find his crackpot ideas. So Tim Boyd would become famous, posthumously, for his precocious observations on *The Odyssey*, only by then it would be too late. By then he would be in the underworld with clear-headed Telemachus. *"Feta* cheese,*"* he would say to him. *"Spanokopita. Se agapo."* (These are the only Greek words Tim knows.)

In his mind's eye he also could see Phoebe, sitting at the back of Dove Chapel during the memorial service, her head slightly bowed.

The paper in his suitcase was like the old man's eye in "The Tell-tale Heart" by Edgar Allen Poe, in case you've ever read it. He held his breath until he was pretty sure that Freddy Goatsucker was asleep and not just fake-snoring so he could surreptitiously pull his pecker under the covers. Then he got up, put on his pants and shoes, and eased the suitcase from under his bed. His roommate whistled once through his big nose, then turned over. Tim opened the suitcase, grabbed his paper, and hurried downstairs, out the front door.

The morning air was freezing. He borrowed a bike that just happened to be leaning against the dormitory. Then, since the Rookery Dorm for Boys is situated on a hill, gravity just wooshed him away from everything that was bothering him. No cars were on the street, except parked ones. The whole downtown was empty, lights changing from red to green the only sign of life. Just before the boathouse he turned left along the river, where kids who rowed crew practiced, and followed it out of town. It was a tidal river, which means it swelled and shrank according to the tides. It also smelled of fish.

Soon he was on the highway, the cold air finding its way to his bare skin. Gray farmhouses and country churches stood silent as he sailed by. Mostly there were just fields, and always in the distance the marshes that showed where the river flowed. He smelled salt even before, huffing and puffing, he pedaled up over the last knob of land, and there, stretching to the sky and beyond—to Murmansk and Arkhangel'sk and Sankt-Peterburg—was the gray Atlantic, its waves coming up onto the shore.

He ditched the bike in some bushes and ran headlong over rocks and sand to the water's edge. Some pages of his paper flew around his head like gulls. The rest he tore up and littered in the lapping waves.

Then there was no paper.

He sat on a rock, hugging himself. He read in a book once

that Indian yogis can bear extreme temperatures simply by denying their existence, but since he was just an ordinary person, he had to use his shirt sleeve to wipe his nose.

This was probably the nadir of his life so far. However, the nadir goeth before the zenith.

He was just sitting there, catching his breath, when the first miracle happened. Where the moon made a silver path on the sea, three barking heads came swimming toward him, their dog noses spreading silver ripples before them. They were sea otters, coming across the cold inhospitable sea to see what kind of creature that was, perched on a rock. Don't laugh. He felt honored, like he was important in the universe after all, whatever other human beings might think. He stood up, laughing and wiping the tears from his eyes.

On the way back to Webber's Pond, Dawn's rosy fingers spread across the sky.[1] But he should have been wearing his coat because it was starting to hurt when he swallowed. He made sure by swallowing again (masochism). Yes—swallow—he had a sore throat. And a splitting headache as well.

That afternoon in Sex and Human Values all the kids were subdued, staring out the window at the first snowstorm of the year. When English was finally over, he ran downtown to get some throat lozenges. He was slip-sliding uphill, trying to make it to the dining hall, when overhead a light went on. That's when he looked up and saw Phoebe, the real her.

■

On the roach coach going home for Christmas you could hardly see for all the *marikhuana* smoke. Even straight kids

[1]Homer, *The Odyssey*, pp. 7, 12, 22, 26, 72, 99, etc.

were barfing Absolut in the aisles, and the poor conductors couldn't do anything about it since many of the kids' fathers and mothers were famous lawyers. Tim stared out the window at all the frozen fields and ponds and piles of junk people had just left by the tracks.

When no one was looking, he breathed on the glass and wrote *Phoebe*, then quickly wiped it out with the sleeve of his brown jacket.

You can be surrounded by people who are acting like jerks and still think anything you want—it's a powerful feeling. He pretended to be asleep, but really he was trying to have a fantasy about Phoebe Sayornis. It was spring, and he was coming up Branch Lane, the little street that went past her house. He had walked up and down this street many times when they let him out of the infirmary, but unfortunately her window was always dark and the shade always down. Some pewit or peckerwood probably had told her never to get undressed with the shade up since there were boys around, and everybody knows what boys are like.

She called to him from the porch: "Tim!"—he could almost hear the way her voice would say it. He stood on the porch steps, talking through the screen. She was on the glider, in shadow. . . .

Unfortunately, that's as far as he got. He couldn't make himself imagine other stuff because compared to other boys his age he wasn't that experienced (i.e., virgin). He tried to kiss the shoulder of his coat, to see what it felt like, but you can't tell.

SprinG

He was sitting on the concrete embankment of the Great Skua River, his arms hanging through the iron railing, smoking a Camel cigarette. He knew that they gave you lung cancer, because far away his grandfather, a heavy smoker, was coughing to death. But he had been subliminally influenced by the Old Joe ads you see everywhere. That guy is the definition of cool, with a cigarette dangling from his camel lips and, in the background, a woman who probably longs to touch his leathery nose and taste his tobacco breath.

His face, if you've ever looked at it closely, resembles the diagram of the male reproductive system found on page 37 of *Smart Sex*, their textbook for Sex and Human Values.

He still didn't know what made a girl like you. Maybe this will work for me, he thought, taking a puff.

He was supposed to be reading a letter from Seryozha, his friend in Moscow, who faithfully sent him soccer scores, plus the latest news, such as life is shit, you wait for hours in line, when you get to the head of the line there's nothing left to buy. In the open markets everything is available, but a pair of jeans costs three weeks' salary.

It was weird to have his two worlds come together like this, albeit briefly. Part of him felt that if somewhere people had to live like that, what was he doing here? But he stuffed the letter in the back pocket of his brand-new Levis. He could read it later.

The evening sky was perfectly reflected in the brimming water so that for a second he was Zeus, hurler of thunderbolts, sitting in the center of the universe. Clearing his throat, he leaned forward and spit as far as he could, saw the shadow rise to a smacking sound, as beneath his glowing Reeboks the sky shivered.

And all the while everything alive seemed to be waiting for something to happen at the bend in the river.

The boys were already hauling their boats up the ramp, laughing and calling, scraping wood against wood. Just before the girls appeared, just as the coxswains' high small voices preceded them around the bend, the light on the river grew a shade darker, there was a moment in the twilight when nobody said anything, there was no sound, no motion—just three long boats gliding up the middle of the river.

In all three boats the rowers reached and pulled in perfect unison. Girls generic, girls perfect, the very Idea of girls. Then Coach Pipistrello—this old bat who teaches Italian—sputtered by in her motorboat, squawking through her bullhorn. Lifting their oars, the rowers turned back into just kids, also girls, but myriad, individual.

And a puff of smoke arose from the greenwillow tree.

In a lot of ways *his* girl—the second one in the second boat—was a rather ordinary-looking person. Just then, for example, she was holding her elbow out so she could pull her shirt away from her armpit. She tilted her mouth up toward the darkening sky so she could blow the hair out of her eyes, then leaned back to hear what her friend and teammate Julie Crake was saying.

It was weird; it was ten times easier to joke around with Julie "Jewels" Crake. Once she has asked him, "So, Tim, who do you like? Or are you gay?" and he said slyly, "Who wants to know?" At the time, Phoebe was standing on the steps, her head slightly bowed.

He liked Jewels *as a friend.*

Why is it that when a girl likes you, she's nice and everything, but kind of on the chubby side, whereas if you like someone, she's probably too good-looking to like you back? What was God thinking when he designed the world this way?

As he sat there, in his sanctuary of long branches and budding leaves, taking manly drags off his Camel cigarette, the girl of his dreams looked to see where Julie was pointing, then turned to say something to the girl behind her.

They were just passing, maybe fifty meters from where he sat, when the whole boat turned in his direction. In scattered voices they sang out, "Hey, Russky, we love your butt!" (That was the in phrase at AP that spring, don't ask me why.) A second later little ripples washed against the shore.

Timur raised his hand and wiggled his fingers. A few minutes later, back in his room, trying to catch his breath, he stared at the book he was supposed to be reading.

■

If you love someone, sooner or later you must tell someone. It's axiomatic.

It rained all day, May 19, his Day of Destiny. The playing fields were so flooded that all the Saturday games were canceled. He wandered into the Old Gym where his dorm brother, Chris Kite, was playing by himself in one of the squash courts, whacking the ball against the front wall.

"Hey, Communist, come in here and get your ass kicked."

It was useless to explain to guys like Chris that he was not a Communist.

Chris had two rackets, so Tim said calmly, "I'll play you." He stepped inside.

At first they just took turns hitting the ball off the front wall. Both of them stunk. Chris hated competitive sports.

He preferred Outdoor Fitness, where, when the teacher wasn't looking, you could go behind a tree and smoke dope. Tim, before he attended AP, thought squash was a vegetable.

Chris said, "I'll play you for your girlfriend."

Tim could feel his heart beating, but he just shrugged and said, "I don't have a girlfriend."

Chris was looking at him, smiling his crooked smile. "Now's your chance. Go ahead, anyone you want. Winner gets to do anything he wants to her, including—" He mentioned words not approved by Sex and Human Values. "Okay?"

Tim looked at him. "Okay," he said. He expected Chris, being such a stud, to mention a sexpot like Judy Nuthatch, but instead, after caressing his jaw for about five seconds, he said, "How about Phoebe Sayornis? Her tits aren't very big—they're kind of high on her chest—but she's got the prettiest face of any girl in your grade."

Tim was staring at the front wall. The air seemed to ring. He felt like hitting Chris with his racket, smashing his wide mouth, but all he said was, "Volley for serve?"

It never occurred to him that someone else would like Phoebe, too.

"One other thing I forgot to mention. The loser has to do it with a teacher. I'm serious. You have to at least try. You can't just chicken out."

"Snipe-Do," Tim blurted, confident of winning.

"She probably would. Volley for serve."

So two boys were in there playing a game of squash to see who would win the girl. It sounds chauvinistic when you stop and think about it, but at the time they were just fooling around. They had nothing better to do.

At first they played nonchalantly, but you could tell that

Phoebe Sayornis was working as incentive because some of their volleys lasted five strokes or more. However, Tim had a secret advantage: there was *no way* he could lose. Whatever it took—crashing into walls, skidding across the floor on both knees—he got the ball.

Probably, though, he shouldn't have run around the court afterward, flapping his arms and crowing. Or put his arm around his dorm brother and said, "You can borrow my good-luck condom if you want. I've only been sitting on it in my wallet for about half a year. By the way, Snipe-Do has a copy of *Dr. Ruth's Sex Guide*—so you'll never run out of ideas for what to do next."

It's true, too. She invited their class to her faculty apartment in Duckworth once, and there it was, in hardcover, for the whole world to see.

Probably he shouldn't have strummed on his racket like a balalaika, singing, "Come to me, Phoebe, my love."

Never in a million years did he think Chris would be such a traitor as to actually tell her. But that night at the weekly dance in the Old Gym, she came up to him with a can of what he thought at the time was Coke, lifted her elbows slightly, and said, *"Ya lyublyu vas."* In case you don't speak Russian, it means I love you.

■

Although Timur came from the land of the black market, where anything and everything are for sale (if you have dollars—rubles are toilet paper), and then lived for four years in New York City, the smut capital of the world, he wasn't so experienced when it came to girls.

At the junior high he went to, kids didn't really date. They mostly went places in groups. The closest he had ever come to doing anything was in the eighth grade once when he went down in the basement of his old building with Geraldine Merganser, a girl he sometimes walked home with. There was a pile of old mattresses in a storage room down there, which they lay on top of for almost an hour, it felt like. Mostly they just listened to each other breathe because Tim was too sickening a chicken to even try and kiss her.

Even so, he was sort of proud of himself. Even now he can't fall asleep at night if he starts thinking about Geri, who was a cute blond with sort of pouty lips and only a few pimples that she put Clearasil on. The jeans she was wearing had holes in the legs, and you could see some microscopic blond hairs in there. If you try to describe it, it doesn't sound like that big a deal, but at the time Tim felt like a musical instrument waiting to be played.

After that they went skating one afternoon at the Columbia rink and held mittens, and she made little skipping movements before gliding out. Unfortunately, before he could get to first base with her, he discovered they didn't have that much in common. She wanted to work in her dad's insurance agency when she grew up, whereas Tim wanted to do something more exciting, maybe be a cosmonaut.

She must have realized at the exact same time that they weren't made for each other, because two weeks after they went down in the basement together, she started going out with Jimm Ruff, who wore sunglasses indoors and out, and played drums in the school band. People said he had seven rings on him, but only three were visible to the naked eye.

Briefly Tim aspired to become a musician, too, but when he blew into his Uncle Lyova's shiny gold saxophone, all that came out was a honk like a spanked duck would make (duck abuse).

He has never told anyone this before—for obvious reasons (he doesn't want them to think he's a geek or worse), except once in the Butt Room he lied and said he'd almost gotten a girl pregnant. He might have, too, if sperms could hop down your pants legs like fleas.

■

Don't ever try to talk over Fresh Road Kill, this band from Portland, Maine, that nobody except the Dance Committee had ever heard of before, because if you do, you won't be able to hear the words that come out of your own mouth, let alone somebody else's.

When Phoebe Sayornis leaned—maybe "lunged" is a better word—toward Tim's right ear and shouted with all her might, "I love you!" what she really said was, "Yellow blue bus."

If you say it fast in English it sounds like "I love you" in Russian.

"Somebody told me to say that," she explained. "Is it dirty?"

"It means—nothing," he said, looking around to see who the traitor was. Chris was standing with the other losers from their dorm. When they saw him looking at them, they began falling over each other with laughter. Freddy made a circle with the finger and thumb of his left hand, then stuck his right finger in.

How immature can you get?

Before he even had time to think about what he was doing, he took Phoebe's hand—she turned out to have an ordinary person's hand, slightly moist—and they walked across the gym floor and began dancing. There were maybe six other couples, not counting the freshman girls who always danced in a group.

He could hardly take in that it was really her. His legs and arms were dancing, but his mind was a stone.

Lights rotated around the gym. They had pulled back the net that usually hung around the indoor tennis courts, and most of the kids just stood there, in the net's shadows. In other words, where he usually stood. He knew what they were thinking: *This* is Saturday night? What supposedly I've been looking forward to all week? Then they probably went back to their dorms and pulled their peckers (or whatever you call it when girls do it) and started doing their homework for Monday's classes.

But tonight Lady Luck was smiling on him for a change.

Phoebe wore her hair up. She had on a black miniskirt, red lipstick, and little silver earrings—tiny hoops of different sizes like miniature planets in orbit around her earlobes. At least that's what he thought until he put his warm face close to hers, and they turned out to be tiny skulls hanging from crossed bones.

For some time he'd been thinking about getting his ear pierced, too, since half the guys he knew wore earrings— but remember, *the right one is the wrong one*. What if at the last minute you made an honest mistake?

Also, she was wearing a blouse without any sleeves so that anybody who wanted could look at her armpits. It may not sound like such a big deal to somebody who has never met Phoebe Sayornis, but if you really like someone, you like their armpits. It's an infallible test, like whether or not you want to lick their teeth.

He kept hoping they would play music he knew how to dance to, since he was mostly just hopping from one foot to the other, sort of making it up as he went along. But the band just went *blam, blam, blam—feedback*, so after about five minutes of healthy aerobic exercise he tugged on her hand and pointed to the exit. She looked at him for about a second, then nodded. First she had to stoop down and get her shoes from where she had kicked them off.

Outside on the ramp there were a bunch of other couples standing close to each other, so they went back inside. Without discussing it, they walked down the deserted corridor that smelled of old jockstraps and had team pictures dating back to time immemorial on the walls. It was dark in there, except for the emergency lights they kept burning at all times. It's hard to say which of them had the idea of stepping over the chairs that had been lined up as a barricade with an OUT OF BOUNDS sign taped to a string, but they did, and the next thing anybody knew, Tim Boyd—who never used to break rules—and Phoebe Sayornis, who everyone *thought* was quiet and shy, had slipped into one of the empty squash courts and shut the thick, insulated door behind them.

■

Now he had to talk to her.

That night in bed, grinning in the dark, he could remember everything they said, plus all the pauses in between, and the way she kept looking at him for about two seconds and then away. But now, half a year later, he mostly remembers sitting on the floor with his back against the wall and her less than fifteen centimeters away, feeling vibrations from the band in the *zhopa*—or buttocks, if you prefer—and picking his Styrofoam cup apart like a flower.

How did the Styrofoam cup get in there? It's one of life's little mysteries.

Probably he doesn't remember more because he's blocked

it out, but unfortunately he does remember reciting some lines from Boris Pasternak, his mother's favorite poet. It made him feel powerful to be saying such tender words to her, which she couldn't understand. But also sad, too.

"Translation?"

"It's saying that when you really love someone, whatever happens you will go on loving them forever."

Phoebe burped and said "Ralph" at the same time.

"Want some?" she said, waving her can in his face.

He took a swig and nearly choked. "This is not Coke," he stated.

"It's not 'Cawk,' " she said, smiling. "It's vodka. I thought you'd like it."

"Oh," he said, looking at her. "I don't drink that much. It gives me a headache. Just at family parties, when there are toasts."

She wrinkled her nose. "I don't, either," she said, looking at him for half a second. "I just carry it around to make a statement."

He said "Oh" again, looking at her from the corner of his eye.

"Oh, shit," she said, "You probably think I'm twelve years old. I personally don't believe in drinking, but I think I should be able to make my own decision. Not because of some dumb rule."

"Fred," burped Tim.

She worked her chin and throat and came up with "Chris."

"Chris?" he burped.

"I personally think love is a crock," Phoebe stated, sniffing her vodka and wrinkling her nose again.

"You do? Why?"

"For personal reasons."

He went cold and clammy all over.

Phoebe sighed. "My parents used to love each other," she said. "Now they sure don't. Also, ever since I was about twelve, half my mom's boyfriends have been hitting on me. I hope you know what that means."

"It means they tried to get in your pants."

"And half of them are married."

"Really?"

"Why, does that shock you?" She looked at him. "Are you religious or something? I personally think that God is just something to make us conform. I used to be an atheist, but now I'm an agnostic, since you can never know for sure. Oh, shit," she said, frowning. "You're probably a believer, right? What are you, Russian Orthodox? Jewish?"

"It's okay." He was smiling. "I'm used to it. A lot of people I know don't believe."

After kind of an awkward pause, she said, "I didn't mean to insult your religion. I have a lot of respect for religion." She said that and burst out laughing. "Sorry," she said, trying to stop. "I'm just in this crazy mood."

"I don't just believe because you're supposed to," he said. He took a deep breath and told her his theory about peaches—about how peaches are so much more juicy and delicious than they have to be just to spread their seeds and make little peach trees that it seemed like Something in the universe was on our side. "I don't, like, believe in an old man with a long beard." She watched him out of the corner of her eye with a serious expression on her face. "You have to like peaches," he said, smiling.

"I love peaches."

At first it was dark in there, but then your eyes got used to the dark, and there was this faint light coming through the skylight—from the supposedly indifferent heavenly bodies. Mostly they just stared straight ahead, but they also took turns looking at each other for about two seconds or more. Except for the aforementioned vibrations from the band next door, it was very quiet in there.

He was wondering what to do next. She was probably wondering the exact same thing, because suddenly he could feel her looking at him with all her might, and the next thing he knew there was a hand crawling up the back of his head. If he hadn't known it was hers, he would probably have thought it was the hairy tarantula Mr. Limpkin, the biology teacher, kept on a shelf in his classroom—like someone had turned it loose in the squash court to discourage kids from doing any S&HV experiments in there.

He looked at her, but she quickly looked the other way, with a stern, almost angry expression on her face, like she had lost something and couldn't find it. She even set her Coke can down on the floor and got up on her knees and started using both hands so she could, like, feel his head better.

"I read this book at my Aunt Bonnie's summer house," she said in a funny voice, like she was talking through clenched teeth, "on phrenology. Have you ever read about it? It's really interesting. Supposedly you can read a person's mind just by feeling the bumps on their head. Also, you can tell their fortune. You don't mind, do you?"

She burst out laughing so hard that Tim got sprayed by Phoebe saliva (yum), but that didn't stop her from calmly and scientifically probing his bumps and running her fingers behind his ears and lightly touching the back of his neck, probably completely unaware of the fire she was spreading. Frowning, she double-checked this one bump he has on the right side of his head, probably his mound of Phoebos.

Unfortunately it had to be a crock, because even though

she gazed at him long and hard, not one of his real thoughts got through. Finally she sat down with a look of disappointment, crossed her arms, and stuck out her bottom lip.

Tim felt his own head to see if he really had bumps. He did. Probably everybody does, only except for bald people their hair covers them up.

"What?" he said.

She shook her head.

"You have to tell me. I'm too naive? I'm a sex fiend?"

She looked at him for maybe two seconds and sighed. "You're a nice—normal boy," she said in a sad voice. Then she sighed again, louder.

"That's bad, right?"

"No, it's good. I always heard Russians were wild men, but you're a good person, Tim. Practically a saint."

"I'm not a saint," he said, saying a swear to prove it (seal in French). He got up on his knees and started feeling *her* head.

He knows, by the way, that this was kind of a strange thing to be doing on your first date—well, it wasn't officially a date. But usually if you want to fool around with someone you don't, like, feel their craniums up.

But at least he was touching her.

"Well?" she said, looking up at him.

"You're a good person, too," he said.

She wrinkled her nose and made a fat tongue.

"*Not* a saint. Also"—he could feel his heart beating—"you're the cutest girl at AP."

"You don't know how to do it," she said, smiling with her mouth slightly open.

"Yes, I do," he said in his bogeyman voice, moving his face toward hers until instead of two eyes she only had one. She backed away and looked at him sideways, sort of questioningly, as if she was listening to a faint noise—or, rather, *not* listening, since that's when they both noticed.

The vibrations had stopped.

If that doesn't seem like a big deal to you, it means you didn't go to a boarding school where on Saturday night you have to check in by eleven o'clock, or else. He turned her wrist to see what time it was by the man's watch she always wore, but already the school bells were starting to ring. Even in there you could hear them: *Bong. Bong. Bong.*

They scrambled to their feet and out the door, down the dark and empty corridor, putting on their brakes slightly to go around the corner, out through the doors and into the night.

There was not a soul in sight. Even the bad kids, even the druggies, were checking in.

They ran as fast as they could to where the path divided on top of the hill. The bells had stopped. Dorm doors were being scraped shut, their bright lights closed inside.

"Wait," he said. He felt like kissing her on both cheeks, but took her hand instead. "I'm not a saint," he growled. She was tugging at his hand, so he let her go, and she went running downhill toward Whippoorwill House. Only her voice, let loose in the night, called out, "Prove it!"

"Tim!" Bob White said the second he pushed open the door.

"Here!" he said, going up the stairs.

The proctor was holding a clipboard, checking off names, and all the guys were flocking around him, going "Yo" and *"Presente"* and many other witty variations on "Here." From halfway up the stairs Tim regarded them briefly with pity.

■

He was up early the next morning, so he could walk by the
house where she lived, but unfortunately her shade was
down, the room was dark. Without at first really thinking
about what he was doing, he started going around to all the
places that for some reason or other he associated with her.
Out to the soccer field, for example, where once, during a
game against Saint Budgerigar's, when everybody else on
the team was at the other end of the field except for him
and the goalie (he played sweeper), he had caught sight of
her on the sideline, in a bevy of girls. Her hands were raised
to her face, and she was jumping up and down and screaming. When the action came back upfield, he made a miracu-
lous save, ending up with his face in the mud, but when he
sat up and casually looked around, she was gone.

Now, as he wandered around the empty playing fields, he
felt the same way: She was gone. What he was expecting,
even he didn't know—that being his kindred spirit she
would be up early, too? She would be here waiting for him?

A flock of geese flew by overhead, honking and flapping
their powerful wings. It wasn't rational, but suddenly he
felt alone. Yellow blue bus—it was just a means of transpor-
tation.

On the banks of the river, forlorn, he pressed the replay
button of their conversation. There she was, grinning, saying she loved peaches. There she was, making his head
tingle with her probing hands.

Before he had time to chicken out, he ran as fast as he
could all the way back to his dorm, went down in the basement, and dialed her number. It rang and rang. Finally someone answered. They said "Hello!" in a very impatient voice,

and unfortunately when he needed it most, his own voice failed him and he chirped, "C-can I speak to Phoebe Say-ornis, please?"

He hadn't worked out what he was going to say—something witty along the lines of, "It's Saint Timofey from the Bible."

"Who?" said the voice on the other end, so he had to take her name in vain by saying it out loud again.

"Phoebe? Jesus, she lives all the way upstairs. I'm going to be late for the Nature Walk."

He could hear everything that happened on the other end: first, pounding footsteps, then the same voice, only smaller, shouting, "Is Phoebe up there? Well, could you see?"

Before he could hear the answer, the same voice was saying, "I know, she was being totally outrageous, I'm like—"

Doors opened and shut. There were more pounding footsteps. Any minute he expected her out-of-breath voice to say, "Hello?" but instead there was just a long silence. For seventeen minutes and forty-two seconds, according to the shitty Timex on his wrist, he stood in the basement with the receiver pressed against his ear, and every time someone's feet came stamping down the stairs to the first landing and the front door banged open, he covered the mouthpiece and said the first thing that came into his head in a loud voice so they would think he was actually talking to someone, only gradually he realized that if she really did come to the phone, she'd be, like, "You mean you've been standing there for seventeen minutes and forty-two seconds?" I.e., Idiot.

So at last he hung up, went and knocked on some doors, to see if anyone wanted to shoot some baskets, but it seemed like the whole dorm was quiet. The halls were empty. The only other person around was Dave Crane, who came to the door in his swimming trunks and a diving mask. Through his snorkel he said he was doing an experiment.

"Where is everybody?"

"They've gone to the Nature Walk. You want to help me with my experiment?"

"I'd like to, Dave, but I have work to do."

He always had work to do, so it wasn't a complete lie.

At first he was pissed. Why hadn't anyone told him there was a school trip? Then he looked: signs were taped on all the bathroom doors and over the urinals.

NATURE WALK
UP EAGLE MOUNTAIN.

SEE THE THRILLING SPECTACLE
OF NATURE COMING BACK TO LIFE.

BRING CAMERAS.
WEAR BOOTS OR SNEAKERS.

Vans Leave from Parking Lot
Sunday, 12:00 Sharp!

It was 12:17. The only car in the parking lot was Snipe-Do's yellow Honda with the license plate that said WOMYN. He wandered around campus, hitting his hand against every tree he met. Hard. There was no heaven above, just low-lying clouds. The world seemed cold and empty. It was the sort of day when you knew you were going to end up pulling your pecker, even though it's the last thing you felt like doing.

■

Konyets—The End.

It would have been *konyets*, too. None of the things that

happened would have happened. Whenever they passed on the quad they would have just looked at each other funny— i.e., what might have been.

From when he said good-bye to her Saturday night until the following Monday afternoon, he didn't see her once, *not one time*, not even by the milk machine in the dining hall, which is where you usually ran into people you hadn't seen for a long time. It's like that at AP sometimes. Even though it isn't one of the big prep schools, like Exeter or St. Paul's, you can go for days without seeing someone.

Then on Monday after algebra there was a letter in his p.o. box. *Dear Phoebe*, it said. Dear Phoebe? he thought. Somebody must have made a mistake.

> I'm sorry I avoided you on Sunday by not going on the Nature Walk with the rest of the school. You have a right to know what's going on. (Please check one.)
>
> ☐ Some of the things you said the other night made me want to barf in your lap. You mean well, but you're very naive about relationships. I feel sorry for you, but not enough to ever want to talk to you again.
>
> ☐ You're okay, but I L O V E _____ (fill in blank), so you can commit suicide if you want (no notes, please).
>
> ☐ I don't know HOW I feel about you, since I'm a boy and my "feeling apparatus has been fucked up by Society" (Ms. Snipe-Dowitcher, Oct. 12). Whoops, please excuse me. I meant to say "intercoursed up," since I'm a saint and never say swears. I think, however, I like you as a friend. Perhaps we can read some Russian poems out loud together some day. I'll call you.

☐ If you don't know YELLOW BLUE BUS after all
the times I sat under the greenwillow tree and
watched your boat come in, then you're dumber
than you look. Frankly speaking, YOU'RE ONE
<u>KHAT</u> GIRL, and all I can think about is kissing
your unwashed toes (just kidding).

P.S. Julie Crake helped me write this, so blame her.

P.P.S. If the answer is the last one, meet me at the
town Laundromat.

P.P.P.S. At 8 o'clock tonight.

■

The school has its own laundry facilities, but usually
clothes you sent out came back two sizes smaller and pink.
Freddy Goatsucker never bothered to send his stuff out. He
just borrowed other people's, especially their underwear,
which his big butt stretched.

On the fourth Wednesday in May Tim slung his pillow-
case over his shoulder and set out to seek his fortune. It was
a balmy night. His sneakers were glowing in the dark. It felt
like he was bouncing, not walking, downhill to town.

The Laundromat was empty, just a row of machines, rocking and humming. It was actually too hot in there. He
dumped his dirty clothes into the only available washer—
the only one that wasn't in use or didn't have an OUT OF
ORDER sign on it—and turned the knob to cold (which was
all they had anyway). Then he went and sat on one of those
plastic seats where you have to be careful the seat part
doesn't come off and impale you in the planet Uranus. Every
couple of minutes he nonchalantly spun around and cupped
his hands to the glass to see out. Right at eight o'clock
somebody was coming—but unfortunately it was the last
person he wanted to see.

Chris Kite stood in the doorway and said, "Pinko! What the fuck are you doing here?"

He acted jittery, like he was high on something, which, knowing him, he probably was. He came over and stood right next to him and said, "That's my seat."

He wasn't afraid of Chris—he just thought he was an asshole. But if he got into a fight it would spoil everything. It was already spoiling everything that that asshole was even there. (Why are people like that?)

"Out of my seat, Roosky," he said.

Tim stayed there as long as he felt like it, but it was a stupid thing to fight over, so finally he got up and said, "Be my guest" and went outside.

Then these other kids he sort of knew, mostly juniors and seniors, came by and said, "What are *you* doing here, Tim?" like it was pretty amazing that he of all people should be washing his clothes at the town Laundromat. They all had laundry bags and boxes of soap and kept laughing and shoving each other off the pavement. Chris knuckled on the window and gestured for them to come inside. He did not look that happy.

Just then Phoebe stepped out of the night. She was with Julie, and in contrast to Chris and his followers, they looked so innocent, so just ordinary, that Tim felt like going up and hugging them both.

He wasn't in a bad mood anymore. In fact, he couldn't help laughing. He felt like a can of "Cawk" that somebody had shaken up and opened the top of.

"What's so funny?" said Phoebe, but she was laughing, too. For some reason she reached her arms out in front of her, bent over, and touched her toes.

Probably they both felt safe with their chaperone (Julie "Jewels" Crake) there.

The three of them started walking along Front Street, past Cormorant's Drugstore—there were lights on inside, but the sign said closed. Woolworth's. The hardware store. Tim tried to think of something to say to Julie, but when they were even with the bandstand, she veered off. Over her shoulder she called back, "Don't do anything I wouldn't do."

For a second he felt guilty because even though she was pleasingly plump, she was still a nice person. She had a pretty face. He just wasn't attracted to her.

The two of them kept walking along Front Street, looking in all the windows. They were the only people out, so it felt a little unreal, sort of like in Drama Workshop when you walk on the stage during a lighting check and say to the invisible teacher sitting in the audience, "I have to go to soccer practice now." Everyone had to take Drama Workshop, but only the in crowd got to act. "If we ever do Chekhov," Mr. Towhee said, "I'll definitely keep you in mind."

When they got to the end of the block, they kept going. Were you not supposed to? As far as he could remember, nobody had ever said. They walked by old houses that real families used to live in but were now mostly lawyers' offices, across parking lots that used to be front lawns, and finally came to the town mill in the most run-down part of town. It was next to a waterfall, where the Little Skua River flowed over a ledge, spilling five meters or so onto rocks below. There it joined the Great Skua and began its journey to the sea. Once upon a time the mill had been a real mill. Historically speaking, it was probably the reason the town existed at all. Farmers came from miles around to have their corn ground. Then the school's founder, Reverend Crossbill Hatch, had a bright idea: Somebody should educate the farmers' sons.

A steel-and-concrete bridge went over the falls. Standing on it you could hear the steady splash below and feel mist on your face. Sooner or later they would probably turn the mill into one of those gift shops that sell junk only tourists buy. But for the time being it was all boarded up and covered with NO TRESPASSING POLICE TAKE NOTICE signs.

Whatever that means. Tim often finds American signs ambiguous. Like, did it mean that police should take notice (please, officers) or was it just a statement of fact (they did take notice, so watch out)? There was a NO STANDING sign in front of the building at Columbia where Tim's dad used to teach part-time. When they first moved from Queens to Manhattan, Tim used to sit on the sidewalk or, if it was wet out, hop around in circles until his dad showed up.

The Town Fathers probably *didn't* want kids from the local prep school using girders from the bridge to boost themselves up so they could climb headfirst through one of the broken windows, their butts wiggling briefly in the moonlight.

Inside it was like they didn't know what else to do, except walk around, open doors, etc. What was left of the roof let so much moonlight in that a person could have read a book in there, if that's what they felt like doing. Phoebe walked over to the window on the river side of the room and boosted herself up onto a ledge. Her feet were dangling out. Tim went and stood next to her. The rocks below glistened in the moonlight. If you fell, you would probably at least break both legs, or maybe crack your head open, but she didn't seem that worried. So even though he isn't crazy about heights, he climbed up next to her, being careful not to look down, his arm hovering behind her back in case she leaned too far forward.

They took turns seeing who could spit the farthest (he

won). You could hardly hear the spit land because the rushing water made so much noise.

"So what are Russian girls like?" Phoebe asked, letting the backs of her sneakers thunk almost inaudibly against the outside of the building.

"Russian girls?"

"I bet you have a girlfriend back in Russia."

"A girlfriend? I left when I was ten and a half."

The moon flashed in her eyes.

"So what do you think of American girls?"

"I like American girls," Tim said, looking at her for half a second. "They're pretty."

Then they both faced the night sky, and Phoebe asked, "Do you ever want to go back?"

"To visit, you mean? Sure. But I'm American now. I like it here."

"I would like to go to Russia, see what it's really like."

Tim felt like saying that maybe some day they could go together, but that seemed *neskromny*. Time out for dictionary check. That seemed immodest, perhaps impudent.

After a long silence that felt like both of them were waiting for something, Phoebe sighed and went to get down. And right when her hand was still on the ledge, and she was feeling for someplace to put her foot, he quickly put his hand on top of hers. It probably doesn't sound like that big a deal, but at the time his heart felt like a tom-tom. She looked at him, but didn't yank her hand away.

So then they had to get down holding hands because he didn't know if he would ever be brave enough to do it again, and sometimes it's better just not to let go. It was the blind leading the blind. They snuck back out through one of the busted-out windows, and when their feet touched solid ground they took off running—in case somebody was calling the cops. TAKE NOTICE. Two kids just climbed out of the old mill. They're probably on dope or—*bozhe moi*—sexually active.

Walking back, more swinging hands than holding them, it felt like they were a couple. He could hardly believe this was happening (to him). It was only when they got in sight of the Laundromat that he remembered his clothes, which of course those assholes had taken out from the washer and hung up on the bushes to dry. His pajama bottoms had a lilac blossom sticking out of the crotch.

I.e., ha ha, very funny.

They quickly let go of each other's hand.

Chris was standing in the Laundromat, talking to some guy in a motorcycle jacket. When he saw Tim and Phoebe, he came scurrying out and sort of lounged up against the side of the building. "What have you two lovebirds been up to?" he said in his high-pitched voice. He could hardly keep from laughing, then he started sputtering all over himself. He used the back of his hand to wipe his mouth.

His bodyguards were there, too, John Coot, Adam Grouse, a couple of other degenerate wannabes.

"Thanks a lot," Tim said sarcastically, gathering up his still-damp underwear.

"Come here a minute—not you, Roosky, her."

"Do I have to?" she said.

"Don't, if you don't want to," Tim quickly whispered in her ear. He hated Chris's guts, not because he was a long-hair—some of his best friends were longhairs—but because he was an asshole.

Chris said, "I just want to talk to her for a second. May I have your permission, please?"

She went around the corner of the Laundromat, and

Chris's bodyguards, who thought they were nonconformists but were really the worst bunch of conformists because they did whatever he told them to, came and stood in the middle of the sidewalk, with their arms crossed like KGB agents. They had stupid grins on their stupid faces. He just shook his head and got the rest of his stuff.

Bells started chiming. In an instant the hooligans turned back into ordinary kids, shouted, "We've gotta go," and took off. Tim went to find Phoebe, but they were just coming back around the corner. Chris was in no hurry because he lived with his mom and could probably check in any time he wanted. Tim wondered briefly what it would be like to have a son like that. If it was your own kid, would you realize how creepy he was?

"I didn't lay a hand on her," Chris said, holding out his skinny hands, as if for inspection. "Swear to God."

"We better hurry," Tim said, not to Chris, but to Phoebe. He took her hand publicly. They probably should have run, but first he wanted to find out what Chris wanted. He was mad at that creep because he was such an asshole, but he was even madder at himself for not being more like his namesake, the original Timur, also known as Tamerlane— the scourge of the ancient world.

Phoebe just shrugged. "Nothing," she said, looking straight ahead. "He's weird."

"What did he say?"

She shook her head. "I don't want to talk about it."

He was so mad at her when she said that that he let go of her hand, sort of pushing it away—even though, in his heart of hearts, he knew it wasn't her fault.

She carefully took his hand again. "He said if I ever wanted to go for a ride in his golden chariot to just say the word." She looked at him and sighed. "Drugs," she explained. "He grew up in this town. This is where he buys them from his townie friends. You didn't know that?"

He shook his head. He felt like an immigrant.

"Everybody knows, but nobody does anything because they're afraid of his mom. Ms. Killdeer says she has some kind of hold over Dunlin. She probably had sex with him and is blackmailing him."

"Get out of here," Tim said, looking to see if she was pulling his leg. He wasn't mad at her anymore. In fact he felt like saying, "I love you"—in English—but all that came out was, "See you tomorrow?"

■

Eight days before the end of school—for the first time in his life, he wasn't counting—a major case came up before the Disciplinary Committee. According to the proverbial grapevine, it was after midnight when Mr. Grosbeak, the faculty member on duty, went to tell some boys on the first floor to quiet down, people were trying to sleep. The laughter and music seemed to be coming from Dave Crane's room. When Mr. Grosbeak knocked on the door, at first nobody answered. He thought he could hear whispers inside, sounds of heavy furniture being moved. By the time he finally got the door unlocked and pushed away the desks and dressers that had been piled in front of it, the room was empty, except for David, who was lying in bed with his blanket pulled up to his chin. When Big Nose made him get up, he was still dressed and wearing shoes.

The window was wide open.

In the closet Mr. Grosbeak found a warm bong and some other suspicious-looking paraphernalia.

Ick claimed that he had been partying alone. "Who would want to party with a geek like me?" he was supposed to have said. It was probably the first and only time in his life anyone had ever asked him to join in the fun, and he wasn't going to rat on his new "friends."

Everyone said he should pull a Pete Rose and deny everything: "I came back from emptying my Fluff jar and found the window open. The only thing I can figure is that aliens from space must have entered my room, unbeknownst to me."

Then it would have been up to the faculty to prove that he was not telling the truth.

Everybody seemed to know who the other partiers were: the Four Horsemen of the Pucker Lips—John Coot, Adam Grouse, George "Microscope" Sheldrake, and Chris Kite. But during the hearing Mr. Grosbeak had to admit he had only seen the backs of three—maybe four—boys, running. It's a well-known fact that from behind human beings tend to look alike. He was trained to be a teacher, not a cop, he said angrily.

The Disciplinary Committee deliberated until late in the afternoon on the day before dismissal. When the seven faculty members finally emerged from the Bunting Room you could tell they weren't happy. Ichabod Crane, who became known in the annals of AP as the kid who was too dumb to stonewall, got the proverbial boot. But, Tim thought, maybe he just didn't feel like going against his own standards so that he could stay at their prestigious school.

There was not enough evidence to punish the others, though they received a severe warning. On the quad, right in front of the teachers, their friends came up to them and gave them high fives.

■

And then the next day the world of school turned out to be just another illusion, like everything else you think will last forever. In the parking lot Tim hugged Phoebe goodbye. He was kind of in awe of her because she started crying. Her face scrunched up and real tears squirted out. He tried to cry, too, but all that came out was a moaning sound, like somebody having trouble going to the bathroom. Perhaps because he was a boy. It was pretty sad to be saying goodbye, especially when things were starting to go his way, but secretly he felt that he had accomplished a lot.

When he looked around, *all* the girls were crying—even the ones who were just hugging other girls. Still, no one had ever cried because of him before, and it gave him a hard-on, God knows why. Actually, if you want to know the truth, she hugged him too long since there was nothing they could do about it and he could hardly breathe.

Summer

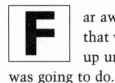**F**ar away a phone was ringing, and he could tell that whoever it was, they weren't going to hang up until someone answered, which no one else was going to do.

His father was asleep in his basement study, with an old fan running—on purpose so he couldn't hear any noises from the hot and humid world above (insomnia).

His mother was in Russia. Grandfather Arkady, the old warrior, had lost his battle with cancer, and his body now lay in the city morgue. Arkady had been a colonel in the Red Army, but after the Soviet defeat in Afghanistan, he had been forced to retire. Overnight he went from a Somebody to a Nobody, and all he and Baboolia had to live on was his pension, which was practically worthless with the recent inflation. When Tim and his parents left Moscow, his grandparents had been glad to sell their nice flat just off the Arbat and move into Boris and Yeva's tiny apartment near the Aeroport metro station. Now, despite all the medals on his big chest, Arkady couldn't find an honorable resting place. The military cemetery at Novodevichy was officially closed to old heroes. Except that maybe with *valoota* (a.k.a. American bucks), Yeva could change a new Somebody's mind.

If the phone was ringing this many times, it slowly dawned on Tim, the answering machine wasn't on. What if his mom was trying to get through? Geez, he thought, whipping his sheet off and running down the two flights of stairs from the attic to the kitchen.

"Allo?" he practically shouted. *"Mama? Kto tam?"*

There was this odd buzzing sound, then a small, familiar

voice on the other end said, "Could I speak to Tim Boyd, please?"

"It's me," he said into the phone. "It's Tim."

"Oh, that's good," said Phoebe, "because that's who I'm calling."

He said, "Where are you?"

"Were you asleep? Wait, what time is it there? Are you ahead or behind?"

"It doesn't matter."

"Where am I? Well, right now I'm at the airport outside of Rome, Italy, but this afternoon I'll be in New York."

"You'll be in New York?" he said, laughing. "This afternoon?"

After a moment's pause she said, "Yes. Bye."

"Wait! Don't hang up!"

But already her voice, which was slightly out of synch, was saying, "So, do you want to, like, do something?"

"Do I want to do something?" said Tim, trying to quick think of something witty along the lines of, does Misha the bear like to shit in the forest? Instead he said, "Where do you want to meet?"

"I think the plane gets in around twelve-thirty or so, but we'd better say two, just to be on the safe side. We're staying at the Plaza, only could we meet someplace else?"

"How about the Met steps? My friends and I used to meet there all the time. The Metropolitan Art Museum—it's just up Fifth Avenue from the Plaza. Do you know where that is?"

"Because otherwise my mom will want to come along. Oh, and I'm supposed to invite you to have supper with us in a restaurant, but we can do something first. What? I can find it, only it might be more like two-thirty. If I'm late, could you wait for me?"

He felt like saying that if it took forever, he could wait for her, but before he could get the words out, something happened to their connection, and then this much smaller voice said, "I have to go now. My mom's jumping up and down and waving. I guess our plane is about to leave. We can only stay until the day after tomorrow, then we have to go home."

There was a brief international pause. Tim was standing there in his underwear, holding the receiver in one hand and his own elbow in the other, and the wire went into this little gizmo on the wall, and outside where it was starting to get light out even though it wasn't officially morning yet, there were telephone poles that went down the hill toward the Staten Island ferry. And somewhere there must have been a cable half in and half out of the water that ran along the ocean floor with little fishies floating around, making bubbles. Or else, since in the West they use satellites for international calls, her voice was probably bouncing around in space. Also, he couldn't help wondering what she looked like in the Rome airport, if she was wearing her spy raincoat, and what expression she had on her face.

She said, "Bye," almost like a question, and he was left holding a dead phone. He went back to bed, but for long time he couldn't fall asleep.

■

He was standing just inside the doors to the museum, listening to muffled booms of thunder and looking out all the windows. On Fifth Avenue the traffic flowed thick and slow: white and blue buses toiled to the curb, then pointed back into the stream. Yellow taxis flitted in and out among them. Every once in a while someone who wasn't Phoebe got out of a taxi and ran up all the stairs. They stood panting for a second or two in the dusky vestibule before shedding their raincoats and joining the crowd inside. The impassive guards took turns walking to the doors, stopping a second, then turning away. Tim examined every coat and umbrella that entered, wondering how much Phoebe might have changed over the summer.

She didn't come and she didn't come and then suddenly it didn't matter how long he'd been waiting (since quarter to two), because there she was, running the way only she ran, up the steps with her legs wide apart, one hand held high above her head like she thought it would keep the rain off her face. At the last minute he pulled the heavy door open, and she marched in, probably thinking they had automatic doors like in a supermarket. In the lobby she looked like a girl you might see anywhere—i.e., not a love goddess.

He went up and touched her on the shoulder. She spun around. For about ten seconds they just stood there, looking each other over, slowly breaking into grins, even though they were both probably thinking, *This* is the person I've been dreaming of morning, noon, and night? (At least he was.)

She held her finger up and after another second went "Whoeeet!" It was a little kid's sneeze, and for some reason people around them seemed pleased. "Bless you," this one lady said cheerfully, but he was worried because her hair was plastered down and her clothes were soaking wet.

"I have to go to the bathroom," Phoebe announced, starting off to find one.

He hurried after her, unbuttoning his shirt. "Here, put this on," he said, sort of draping it over her head. "You'll catch cold."

She disappeared into the ladies' room with it still on her head.

Giving her the shirt off his back wasn't that big a deal

since underneath he had on his sexy WHAT HAVE *YOU* DONE
FOR PERESTROIKA? T-shirt with a picture of Gorbachev.

When she came back out seconds later (so why did it take
his mom so long?), tucking in the tails of his favorite blue
shirt, her own shirt wadded up in a ball, it was like a con-
firmation that they were more than just friends. Now probably he could hug her if he wanted to, since he would just be
hugging his own shirt. On her, though, it looked completely
different. It made her eyes look so blue, you had to look
twice to make sure they weren't brown or black. He couldn't
stop looking. His lips were dry from licking them so much.

■

"You want to see my favorite painting?" he said. It was by
Jan Vermeer, a Dutch painter of the seventeenth century.
He had discovered it earlier, while he was walking around,
killing time.

Phoebe looked at him. "Tim," she said patiently, the way
you talk to a mentally challenged person, "you don't really
want to look at paintings, do you?"

"What else is there to do?"

"It's nice out," she hinted.

Just then thunder exploded over Central Park and the
lights flicked on and off.

"You want to go out in the rain?"

"Oh, that's a good idea!" she said brightly.

"We'll get soaked," he said. He could feel the dumb smile
that had set and dried on his face.

She kept nodding eagerly—as if to say Yes! Yes! Let's!—
but a couple of seconds later, when they were standing
under the waterfall that spilled from the roof, and he
shouted, "So where do you want to go?" she looked at him
like she wasn't so sure after all.

"Do *you* want to?" she said. She had to say it twice because the rain was making so much racket.

Theoretically they could have just turned around and gone back inside, where it was nice and dry, and he could have showed her his Vermeer—see if she agreed that it looked a little like her, at least the cheeks—but at the time it was as though they had already made one of those irrevocable choices they were always talking about in Sex and Human Values. So he nudged her with his shoulder and, leaning toward her ear, which he suddenly felt like biting (not hard), shouted, "Let's go—that way."

So they stepped out into a world of water.

They went down the steps slowly, matter-of-factly, not making a dash for it the way people usually do when it's raining out, and when the light changed they just calmly walked across the street like there was nothing unusual about blowing raindrops off your own lips. After a while, you got used to it. It wasn't good or bad, just different. Madison Avenue was also car-logged. Probably because of the rain, the honks of cars and cabs sounded almost musical. Whenever a driver slammed on his brakes, a pink halo rose in the mist.

Rain plinked off Timur's nose. His shoes were heavy with water.

"I feel like a clown," he said in a loud voice, as they traipsed across 83rd Street. The apartment buildings around them looked like tiered ships ready to sail away. "Look," he said, "we're leaving tracks." Walking backward for a while, they watched their footprints disappear in the rain. "What time is your mama expecting us?" The rain had picked up, so he had to say it again, shouting.

"It doesn't matter."

"Will she be pissed that we're all wet?"

She looked at him and shook her head.

"She'll probably be pissed at me," he said. "We can't go to a restaurant like this."

"So? We can eat in our room. Quit worrying. I'll fix you something. We have a little kitchen." She looked at him again. "Do you like chicken noodle soup?"

"I love chicken noodle soup."

"I can make us some."

They crossed Park and Lexington Avenues. In the museum she had seemed bashful, which made him feel that way, too, but walking in the rain seemed to uninhibit her—if that's the correct phrase—and that gave him the courage he needed. He reached over and took her hand. They had held hands before, so this was like picking up where they had left off, but just to be on the safe side he sort of swung it at first. That way if she'd been having second thoughts in Italy and yanked it away, he could act like he was just fooling around, like it was no big deal. But she didn't (yank it away), she just looked at him and then away for the hundredth time.

So they went on shouting to each other over the racket of the rain like nothing had happened, but mostly he was aware of holding her slightly-warmer-than-room-temperature hand.

A bedraggled bird flew in front of them and landed under an awning. They kept on going. The wind blew the rain sideways for a while. It seemed to be letting up. From the river came the absentminded rumble of old thunder. Then the rain started coming down harder than ever, and spouts rose from the sidewalks like little silver flowers. There were only about two other people out in the rain, but they were making a dash for it. They weren't smiling so hard their cheeks almost hurt. Most people just waited under awnings or in doorways for it to let up.

It seemed like the city was theirs. They could do anything they wanted.

And then, it was like he didn't know how they got there, but they were standing over the agitated water of the East River, their hands right next to each other on the iron railing. Gracie Mansion was on the left, the Queensboro Bridge on the right. Farther down there were other bridges in a sort of tangle. A helicopter with lights on its head and tail labored upriver, while out on the water tugboats plied noiselessly among some tankers. Rain danced on the waves like sardines; under their feet the old gray waves sloshed against the concrete parapet.

They started leaning over the railing and shouting things that nobody besides them could hear, which cracked them up at the time. They kept laughing and shivering and shouting and pointing, and their faces kept coming closer and closer together. For some reason he didn't feel shy anymore. It's hard to feel shy when you can see a girl's breasts in your own blue shirt.

"Look." She pointed.

He put his arm around her wet person and was surprised by how solid she felt. "I see," he shouted. "A flying saucer."

She stepped against him. They were both pointing in the same direction.

His heart was surging in rhythm with the waves. "That's the twelfth flying saucer I've seen this year," he managed to say, even after it turned out to be an airplane with a flashing tail.

She looked at him sideways, but said, "My Aunt Bonnie saw one on Cape Hatteras once. Everyone was standing in the ocean and someone said, 'Look, a flying saucer!' There really was one. It made a whistling sound like this—" Phoebe tried to whistle, but nothing came out. "I'm serious," she said, frowning. "They had an article in the paper."

She turned her face up to his. (She had a chicken-pox scar on her forehead.) He had both arms around her now. "They even quoted my Aunt Bonnie. You don't believe me?"

He kissed her wet face. Unfortunately at the time he still thought you were supposed to make the kissing sound, but it was raining so hard she probably didn't hear.

"I'll show you if you ever come to visit me," she said, when he leaned back to look at her.

If you want to know the truth, the moment he had been looking forward to with such dread and longing seemed so much more—natural—than he expected. Also she had the darkest blue eyes he ever saw in a human face. Her wet hair only made them look darker.

"I believe you," he mumbled before kissing her again. This time she stood on her tiptoes, to help. She pressed her lips against his and—if it's not too personal—put her tongue in his mouth. He had heard of people doing that, though he had never understood why you would want to (before).

The only thing is that right in the middle of kissing her, he felt alone. He wondered if she did, too. You can put your tongue in somebody's mouth and not give a damn about whether you catch their microbes or not, and vice versa, and still not know what they are thinking. When they stopped, which they had to after a while, to breathe, they both turned back to the railing and stared at the river.

At first neither of them said anything. A slight wind, blowing at their backs, gave the water goose bumps. Through a chink in the clouds, the sun began shining.

Finally he couldn't stand it anymore, so he blurted, "I kissed you."

She lowered her eyes slightly and said something he couldn't hear at first, so he said, "What?" and she shook her head and said it again: "I know."

They stayed to watch the light of day resume around them. The sky went back up where it belonged, color reappeared all over the river, New York was once again the fifth largest city on earth, and they were standing there in wet clothes.

■

On the subway Phoebe had a worried look. "I have to warn you. My mom thinks we're, like, practically going together, so just humor her, okay? After supper we can sneak out and do something. You want to go up to Hartsdale and see my dad?"

Tim just looked at her.

"I know, I know," she said. "He comes across as kind of a show-off when he gets up in front of an audience. But it's just an act. He's really hilarious, when you get to know him. You can't stop laughing. Only don't tell my mom we're going or she'll flip."

Tim didn't say anything one way or the other. He was busy examining her hand, like he'd never seen one before.

He personally had never been in the Plaza, except when he and his friends were being rowdy and taking a shortcut through the lobby, and he felt a little funny, because the uniformed guards kept looking at him like they could tell he didn't belong there (paranoia). It's a very fancy hotel, with gold wallpaper and chandeliers, but nobody said anything. They're probably used to bratty rich kids.

He had never thought about it before, since to him all

Americans were rich, but in the elevator when he took a good look at her, he realized Phoebe had to be really rich to be staying in a place like this. What would she think if she saw their house on Staten Island that was supposed to have personality, only if people say that about a house or a girl, look out (it means they're ugly).

Needless to say, Phoebe started quacking like a duck and pretending it wasn't her, which cracked them both up at the time, though nobody else seemed that amused, except for the Spanish elevator operator who, when he opened the door for them with a flourish, said "Eleventh floor" in a Donald Duck voice.

By the way, Donald was an old friend of Tim's. When he and his parents first came to this country, they spent hours sitting in front of a television, watching Walt Disney cartoons and "Sesame Street." Boris was convinced it was the best way to learn American culture and language at the same time.

"Hurry, Mom," Phoebe said, pounding on the door to their suite. "I have to go—bad!"

The door was opened by a woman with one of those tans only rich people get, plus about eighteen silver bracelets tinkling up and down both arms. Phoebe rushed past her and Tim was left shaking her cool hand. He made the mistake of calling her Mrs. Sayornis.

"Not Mrs. Sayornis," she said coolly in a Southern accent (she was from Tennessee). "So this is the other little love-bird. Why are kids in such a hurry to grow up nowadays? Enjoy your childhood while you can—you've got the rest of your lives for heartbreak."

"Yes, ma'am," he said, wondering what exactly Phoebe had told her.

The room didn't look like any hotel room he had ever

been in before—well, he had only been in two, one in Yalta, for a vacation, and one in Vienna, en route to the USA. But this was more like an apartment. Where you first went in, there was a little living room with mirrors in fancy frames, so dark you could hardly see yourself, plus one of those console TV sets that old people in Brooklyn have.

He felt a little guilty, because less than an hour ago he had put his tongue in her daughter's mouth and vice versa, but he decided to act like he knew what he was doing (i.e., rich). He said, "So how was *Italia*?" and smiled his Bob-White-Senior-Proctor smile, but she went, "Excuse me, honey, I'm on the phone."

■

He doesn't wish to say anything bad about Not-Mrs.-Sayornis. He has since thought about what it would be like to be Phoebe's mom and doesn't envy her. She was nice-looking, if you like ladies that age. Also, she kept trying to be a good mother, like when she got off the phone she said they both had to take showers because Phoebe kept holding up her finger and sneezing.

Unfortunately their luxury suite had *two* bathrooms (smile).

Tim used Phoebe's. He felt funny because her drugstore items were spread around for all the world to see. Also, half her clothes were draped on the shower rack. Just as he was getting undressed, the door opened and Phoebe slipped in. She stepped into the tub—it was a big old-fashioned tub with claws—and stood there, arms folded. "Keep going," she whispered, "I want to watch." Luckily her mom called to her to quote unquote leave the poor boy alone.

"He can hand his wet clothes through the door," she said.

Phoebe glared at him, but left.

At first, taking his shower—i.e., standing completely naked in his girlfriend's bathroom—he could hardly believe it was his life he was living. Then through the thick walls he heard shouts and the sound of something breaking. He switched off the water and stood shivering. "Slut!" Phoebe's voice said. Tim quickly turned the water back on.

It occurred to him he didn't really know this girl so well. At school she acted shy; here in New York she seemed more rebellious.

When he emerged twenty minutes later with comb tracks in his hair and wearing the only thing he could find—a terry-cloth bathrobe with the hotel's insignia emblazoned on the front pocket—he found Phoebe sitting on the couch, pouting. She was pretending to watch Oprah Winfrey.

"Wow," he said. "I would have least expected *opera* in a hotel like this. Get it?"

Phoebe looked at him, and slowly shook her head, like she felt sorry for him. She was dressed in white painter pants and a green silk shirt with a sort of jungle design on it. Inside you could see the real her, alive and moving (no bra). She mentioned that that's what she and her mother were discussing—"in case you heard anything." Her mother said that this shirt was too revealing, which was "a disgusting thing to say," stated Phoebe. "I'm not a twelve-year-old. Besides, she's no one to talk."

Pretty soon the bell rang—it was room service, just like in the movies. A Spanish lady, looking at him as if she knew something he didn't, handed him his clothes, all neatly folded with his underwear discreetly tucked inside his blue shirt. But when he went in the bathroom to put them on, the jeans felt a little tight in the crotch.

When he came back out, there was a little table that hadn't been there before, set with two places, and it sure wasn't chicken noodle soup on the blue-and-gold plates.

"I hope you like lobster salad," Not-Mrs.-Sayornis called from Phoebe's bedroom, where she was getting dressed, too. "It was either that or gourmet cheeseburger—whatever that means. They probably use imported goat's cheese."

He sat down, and Phoebe came and joined him. Without taking her eyes off him once, she sank her teeth into her sandwich and then deliberately chewed with her mouth open. With her mom around, he noticed, Phoebe did act like a twelve-year-old.

For some reason he was starved. Food had never tasted so good.

Then the telephone rang and Phoebe got up to answer it. She wrinkled her nose and stuck out her tongue but said in her nicest voice, "Hi! You, too. I'll tell her you're here."

"Tell him I'm on my way," Not-Mrs.-Sayornis called from her room, and half a minute later she emerged, dressed like someone in the movies.

That's it, they were like people in the movies, whereas he was more like someone in the audience who, sooner or later, would have to go back out to the street.

She turned around so they could say how nice she looked, and then smiling the sort of smile you smile when someone is taking your picture, she said the sorts of things American mothers probably always say, "Don't just watch television. Why don't you go out to a movie or something? Now that the rain has stopped, get some fresh air."

To which Phoebe, leaning out the door after her, said all the things all American daughters probably say to their single moms: "Bye. Have fun. Don't worry about us. Stay out as late as you want," etc., etc., while with her hand that was still inside the room she kept churning the air (i.e., hurry up and leave).

Then—dum dum de dum—she shut the door.

■

Out in the hall the elevator doors swooshed shut. Phoebe fastened the little chain very carefully. Then, clapping invisible chalk dust off her hands, she came tiptoeing straight at him and plopped down on his lap so suddenly that he didn't have time to swallow, much less wipe his mouth, before she was kissing him again. But after a while she sighed, got up, and went to sit down at her place so she could stare at him while he ate.

She wasn't that hungry, she said, pushing her plate across the table, so he ate her lobster salad, too, but she hogged more than her share of the chocolate cheesecake.

After that, needless to say, they had a burping contest. Then Phoebe got up and found the oldies-but-goodies station on the radio. With a flick of the wrist she turned off the lights.

Every song that was playing on the radio that night seemed to be about them.

Probably nobody else wants to read about stuff like this, and because of what happened afterward Tim almost doesn't want to even think about it again, let alone remember everything in detail, but Boris always says it's better to remember the good with the bad. Whether he wants to or not, Tim remembers everything.

They stood there like they were going to dance, only instead they collapsed onto the luxurious sofa which it took forever to sink into, and the only light, besides the LED display of the radio, was New York City out the open windows.

For maybe ten seconds they just looked at each other, like they were drawing each other's portraits. Then she said, "Teach me Russian."

He had to clear his throat. "What do you want to know?"

"The bad words."

He put his hand out and touched her nose, which she wrinkled when she added, "How do you say fuck?"

"*Nos.*"

"*Nos* is how you say fuck?"

"No, it means this little thing you breathe through."

"*Nos,*" she said, gripping his wrist.

"*Glaza,*" he whispered, touching her eyelids, feeling her eyes twitching underneath.

"*Glaza,*" she repeated, opening them as soon as he took his fingers away.

"*Rawt.*" He put his fingers on her smiling lips, walked them into her mouth. She bit them, softly at first, then harder.

"Rot!?"

"It means mouth. I like your mouth maybe best of all."

She was watching him, without once taking her eyes away, slowing shaking her head, breathing slowly, as if she couldn't believe it was real, which was how he felt, too.

"Now me," she said, twisting up on the sofa so that she was kneeling above him. "*Nos.* Rot?"

"Close."

"That's all I remember. Now I'll give you an English lesson—pretend you don't know. This stuff is your hair."

Hmm, he assented.

"You have to say it—hair."

"Khair," he said, exaggerating the Russian *kh* sound on purpose.

"Softer *h.*"

"Hair."

"Good boy. You learn fast. Let's see, these are your eyes. Can you say eyes?"

"Ice?"

"No! Can I ask you something? You look Russian, except for your eyes, because they're, like, sort of slanted? Like there's someone in there looking out. Do you know what I mean? Are you insulted?"

"No, not insulted. There is someone—me. I'm part Tartar. It's like for all you know you may be part Indian."

"I doubt it. My ancestors came over on the Mayflower. Moving right along, this is your chest." She patted it all over and sighed a big sigh.

It looked for a second like she was going to continue her explorations, but instead she sank down next to him with her head against his aforementioned chest and her hands in her lap. For several seconds neither of them moved. If formerly Tim had a voice, it was no longer there. Phoebe continued to sigh, each sigh louder than the one before. So then his brain shut off; some other kind of intelligence took over. When he touched her breasts, which were right there in her silk shirt, she twisted away, shy, but when he put his hand sort of experimentally on her lap and pressed hard, she practically climbed on top of him and kissed him so hard their teeth clicked and they toppled over sideways.

In other words Tim actually made out with a girl, and without giving a blow-by-blow description, it amazed him that for every action there was an equal, opposite reaction. He had imagined that a girl would be soft and pliable, but in places she was hard, muscular, full of power.

At eight o'clock sharp someone (fate?) knocked on the door. They also rang the bell.

"Oh, shit," Phoebe said, jumping up. Quickly she went

around, turning on the lights and looking at herself in the mirrors that were too dark to see into. "It's my mom."

But it wasn't. It was room service again, the same Spanish lady and a black man this time. They said they had instructions to clear up at eight. It only took them a minute to put everything on a tray and turn the table back into an end table a third its size. Then they left.

But the spell was broken. He wasn't sure why.

Phoebe had just stood there the whole time, looking large and awkward, like she had just gotten up from a nap. After they left, he proposed turning the lights back out. She let him kiss her cheek and the side of her neck, then slipped away.

"My mom's going to be back any minute. I *don't* want to be here." She came up and kissed him, a "please" kiss. "Let's go somewhere. We can go see my dad."

■

If just a few minutes ago you have been half sitting, half lying on a couch with your unforgettable delight, it's hard to understand why suddenly you are out on the street with people milling about, carriages offering to take you for a ride in Central Park. Well, except that in New York City everything is unreal after dark. They started walking down Fifth Avenue, past buildings like palaces. In the Doubleday bookstore imaginary people stood at cardboard counters, browsing through blank books. They were just there so the world would appear to be real and tangible, but it was really just a dream—whose?

Phoebe stopped at the first empty phone they came to. Although he waited at a polite distance, anyone within a three-meter radius could hear her calling out, "Dad? It's me. Someone? Please pick up the phone. Marjorie? It's, like, a

little after eight. Did you get my letter, I hope? I was thinking of coming up tonight—if that's okay—because we're
only staying two days, and you have to meet my friend."
She shot him a look, almost smiled, and added, "I'll call
back in a half hour, okay? Please be home. Thanks. Bye."

She took his arm like they were grown-ups and they continued gaily walking downtown. She still wore her silk
shirt, which seemed to give off squints of light, but she had
put on panty hose and a short skirt and cute shoes—he will
probably never recover from having sat there the whole time
and watched. Over her shoulders she had spread a black
shawl of her mom's. She looked like a Mexican girl in a
what-do-you-call-it?—a mantilla.

They walked all the way to the Empire State Building—
namely from 59th to 34th Street, which is twenty-five city
blocks—but with Phoebe by his side the next thing he knew
practically they were standing in line for tickets to the ob-
servatory, and it so happened that a group of Russian tourists were waiting in front of them. Phoebe kept trying to get
him to say something to them, but he didn't feel like it.

In the elevator Phoebe leaned back against him and, twisting her head around, kissed him on the lips. The Russian
lady, who wore an imitation leather coat, said, "Oy, you see
that? Right in public, too."

"American kids," said one of the men who was with her.
He had a perfect part in his hair, like a former KGB agent.
"No culture. All they think about is sex."

At the 80th floor they entered a second elevator, which
took them to the top. No sooner had they stepped over the
metal threshold than they were standing under the night
sky. From somewhere came a quiet, steady hum. The light
of the city seemed to light up the sky, instead of vice versa.

Let the record show that on the windy side of the observation deck he put his arms around her, and, in between kisses, looked into her eyes, as if all the mysteries in the universe were there, looking back at him. According to their Sex and Human Values teacher, you're supposed to have long conversations about birth control, safe sex, and other human values, if you want to have a meaningful relationship, but at the time simply looking at each other and *not* saying one word seemed like a better idea. You don't always have to talk to communicate.

He could feel people's eyes on the back of his head and hoped it was the Russians. He felt proud that they had taken him for an American kid. Better than proud: He felt like he was on top of the world.

Every few blocks, on the way back to the hotel, Phoebe stopped to use the phone. "Dad," she kept shouting. "Will somebody please answer the phone?"

She dragged him all the way to Grand Central Station, where they had to step over all the homeless people stretched out on the floor, and found where you bought tickets to Hartsdale. But after standing in line for five minutes, she was the one who decided this was crazy. It was after eleven o'clock.

"Maybe they're not home. The mail service between Italy and America is lousy. He probably hasn't gotten my letter yet. Besides, he's a workaholic. He's probably out partying with some big author. I can call him in the morning."

Tim didn't say anything, but he had his doubts. If *he* was Phoebe's dad, he would know when she was coming to town. He would have gladly ditched his big author to spend a night on the town with his one and only daughter. Frankly speaking, he wasn't so sure he admired Goshawk Sayornis as much as she did.

But he was willing to go anywhere she wished.

Somehow, however, they ended up back at the Plaza. He waited in the hall while she went in to see if her mom was back yet. She was; she was in bed already.

"With *him?*" he wanted to know, more curious about such questions than he used to be.

"No!" she said, smiling her shocked little girl smile, as though he had just said the most preposterous thing in the world. "She says he's a prick and a son of a bitch," she reported cheerfully.

She talked softly through the door, which she held slightly ajar. Then, glancing behind her, she came all the way out to where he was standing. She looked up and down the hallway. Before disappearing behind the closed door for the night, she butted up against him and gave him one of those kisses that are like a magic spell, so that even though he was frustrated (blue balls), he went home—by subway and ferry, it took over an hour—in a mist of intoxication.

■

There were three messages on the answering machine when he got home: whispers and heavy breathing (i.e., all from her). While he was playing them back, the phone rang again.

"You're crazy."

"Sh, my mom's sleeping. I forgot to ask you something. Tim, do you, like, like me?"

He wanted to say, "I love you," but he had never said it to anyone before (except his parents). So he said, "Sure, why?"

"Oh," she said. "Phew. More than anyone else at AP?"

"Sure."

"More thaaan—Julie?"

"I just like her as a friend," he started to explain, but she breathed against the mouthpiece like it didn't really matter.

"That's all I wanted to know," she said. "See you tomorrow."

"Wait, Phoebe, do you like *me*?"

"Yellow blue bus."

"Meet you on the Met steps?"

"Tim—can I ask you something kind of personal, and you won't be pissed? Because we don't have much time. Tomorrow's my last day, then I have to go home—fart. You're a virgin, right? Do you, like, want to lose it? With me, I mean." She quickly added, "We don't have to, if you don't want to. I am, too." In a whisper, "A virgin."

When he didn't answer right away because he was having a heart attack, she said, "Oh my god, I'm so embarrassed."

"I—" he said.

"Tim, please. Forget I said anything. I was talking about virgin *trees*. Are you in favor of saving the virgin trees in the tropical rain forests? That's what I meant to ask."

"I want . . ."

"But?"

"Where would we go?"

"But you would want to—if we could find somewhere?"

"I want to, with you. . . ."

■

She told her mom she was spending the night at Sarah Shrike's apartment at 86th and Lex. She called first to make sure it was okay with Sarah. That way, if her mom just happened to call there, Sarah wouldn't be, like, Who? I haven't seen her since school let out.

Little details like that can trip you up, like when Raskolnikov got blood on his clothes.

Sarah was cool. Phoebe didn't have to tell her everything—or at least that's what she told Tim.

He casually mentioned to his father, who was down in the basement, typing on his word processor, that he and a friend from AP were going camping, he wasn't sure where. "So don't think I've been mugged."

His father looked up and smiled. "Haf fun!" he said.

What did his smile mean? He knew?

Even though he had made this trip across New York Harbor dozens of times, he stood in the bow of the Staten Island Ferry with the setting sun warm on his left cheek and made believe that he was coming down from the sky feet first. Boy from Mars returning to earth.

It wasn't so hard to imagine, since the water was a long blue sheet, slightly wrinkled.

She was sitting on the museum steps, and at first she would hardly look at him, let alone talk. They took one of the white and blue buses, but forgot to get transfers, and the driver was one of those assholes who wouldn't give you one after you were already on, so they had to walk through Central Park at dusk. It's supposed to be a jungle in there. On Russian TV they used to always have pictures of the exploited underclasses committing crimes in Central Park. On this day, however, there were just kids playing baseball. Maybe the muggers were still having supper or something.

They hiked up Broadway all the way to the Ping Sing restaurant, and it wasn't until Tim had splurged and ordered all his favorite dishes that Phoebe casually mentioned she didn't like Chinese food. It gave her diarrhea.

"It's okay, I'm not that hungry."

Not even a fat person could have eaten all the food that the waiter brought, which cost Timur three days' wages from painting the garage. He wished she'd said something when he was ordering, but he didn't want to make a big deal of it. He ate and ate, and still the platters were full. Finally he couldn't manage another bite. For the first time in his life, he folded his chopsticks, defeated.

All through the meal she held her teacup in both her hands and watched him over the rim.

Back outside, the city was changing into night. As the evening slowly descended through the trees, the green of the traffic lights on Broadway seemed to clash with the neon sky. They killed time by going up to the Columbia campus. Phoebe was a shadow on the big sundial they have up there, putting both hands out for him to pull her up. You could tell it was her by her foxfire teeth.

"We don't have to do anything we don't both want to," he said casually, like it had been his idea all along. Which it had, he just never thought it would happen.

He still had all the keys to his old building (criminal instinct), so getting in was no big deal. While they were standing in the brightly illuminated lobby, the door to the elevator opened, and old Mrs. Vogel slowly got off, using two canes to walk.

Tim held the button for her.

"How are your mother and father, dear?" Mrs. Vogel said, twisting her Ben Franklin head up at him. "Such nice people."

"They're fine," Tim's head replied. It was sticking out the elevator doors. Some dark-haired girl who acted like she'd never seen him before had scurried on ahead of him.

On fourteen the hall was empty. They ran up the stairs to the roof door. At first he thought they had changed the lock, and that they would have to go to a movie and make out in the back row, which in a way would have been a relief, but you just had to feel your way, jiggle the key a little, and then there was nothing overhead but the evening sky. The door closed behind them with a dull *clank*.

■

Where the door came up, it looked like there was an *izba* made of bricks—what do you call a little house in the woods? Where witches live? It wasn't really an *izba*, just how the top of the stairs looked from the outside. The building's roof was tarred and sloped at the edges, probably so the rain wouldn't collect in a big puddle. He wasn't that afraid of heights, but you instantly felt something. He was glad they had an old water tank up there, something higher than them.

Incidentally, this tank had his name spray-painted on its potbelly—he used to worry he would get in trouble for writing it, but never did. Needless to say, she wanted to add her name, too, but all she had was a ballpoint pen, and in that light you couldn't see what she wrote. Which, knowing her, was probably just as well.

In his backpack he had everything they needed: clothesline, sheets and a blanket, a poncho that folded up into the size of a wallet, two spoons, a fork which they could share, his sheathed hunting knife from Finland. He tied one end of the clothesline to the bottom of the ladder that went up the water tank and the other to a metal object which was sticking out of the *izba*. Then he hung a sheet over the clothesline and put chunks of concrete he found to hold down the sides so that it looked like a tent. Getting down on all fours he unrolled the heavy blanket, and after that he fixed his little flashlight with a top that unscrewed so you could put it down somewhere and have a miniature lantern.

Phoebe acted the whole time like she had no idea what that boy was doing. When he went to get her, she was standing on the wall that formed the edge of the roof with her back to him. "Look," she said, trying to scare the shit out of him.

He put his arms around her. Her body was all rigid, then she leaned backward into his arms. She was heavier than she looked (not fat, though).

It's probably not a very sexy thing to say, but now that there was nothing stopping them, she seemed—not like a stranger, the way she had when he first kissed her—but more like someone he knew too well, like his cousin or something. He couldn't believe he had any right to her.

She also looked kind of carsick—not that she was gagging or anything like that, but her face was a pale moon. It's probably a good thing she didn't eat any Szechuan shrimp with garlic sauce.

They strolled around the roof, arm in arm, stopping in all the corners to spit over the side. Down on the streets below there were the usual cars, people going places. A piece of paper floating in the air turned out to be a bird, spread its wings, and flew away.

The darker it got, the more the blue tent seemed to glow.

Finally they got down on their hands and knees and crawled inside. At first they acted as if they were doing *anything but*. They kept at least some of their clothes on until almost the last minute. (It was only *afterward* that she wanted to dance naked in the moonlight.)

Everything took longer than he expected because he kept hurting her without meaning to. "Ow," she said, giving him a heart attack.

Her eyes watched him the whole time, and she breathed

through her mouth, probably because of a slight cold, which you could faintly smell. After a while she started smiling with her lips open, dreamily, but then made another face.

"Tim, this is not going to work."

But in his heart of hearts he knew it had to.

Sometimes people talk about making love as if it's something sacred, like a person's mantra. Other times, like on TV, it doesn't seem like that big a deal. In reality it was neither one nor the other. It was like going on a trip with someone to a place neither of you had ever been before.

It would be an invasion of privacy to tell what Phoebe Sayornis looked like when she had kicked the last of her clothes off, but to speak generally there came a time when there was simply nothing more to be embarrassed about. Nobody of the opposite sex had ever seen him completely undressed before (at least not since he was a little kid). Nobody period had ever seen him with an erection.

He felt like Superman with his blue cape on.

Not to worry, by the way. They had gobs of protection, too much, if you ask him. She still had her S&HV condom in a white paper bag. It said *Cormorant's Drug, For All Your Family Needs Since 1954.* Inside was the sales slip, in case they decided to ask for their money back.

A sperm would have had to be Penn and Teller to get through.

Afterward he felt proud and hungry.

"Let's get dressed and go get a cheeseburger."

"Eat this," she said, sitting up and rummaging through her purse. She handed him a peach, slightly mushed on one side. As he ate it, she started singing, softly at first, then louder. She said it was a Shaker hymn.

"'Tis the gift to be simple,
'Tis the gift to be free."

She wanted him to sing and dance with her, but he preferred to suck his peach pit and watch.

Leaping around on the rooftop, under the light of the moon, she was Isadora Duncan, wife of the Russian poet Sergei Esenin, who wrote his last poem with his own blood.

Afterward, lying side by side, they couldn't stop talking, like kids at a sleepover. It was as if each of them wanted the other to know everything about him. Or her.

Incidentally, they don't have this custom of sleepovers in Russia. A couple of summers before, when the kid upstairs had asked him if he wanted to spend the night at his apartment, Tim had said, "Why?"

Phoebe asked him a hundred questions about what it felt like to leave Russia and come to America and what his first impressions were and if it was hard to make new friends, and when he tried to answer her, she listened and asked more questions.

When it was her turn, she told him the story of her life, too, how according to her mom her dad secretly hated women, but she (Phoebe) thought he *loved* women (just not her mom). And once when they were on a trip somewhere and had stopped for gas, she got out of the car to use the ladies' room, and when she came back out, the car was gone. Luckily the gas station attendant wasn't a serial killer. "If it had been television, and not real life," she pointed out, "he would have been." Instead, he gave her salty peanuts and a Coke and let her sit on his desk and write bills on his bill pad. It was her first Coke— maybe that was the point of the story? When her parents realized their mistake and came back, they were still arguing.

He was interested in everything she said, but frankly speaking he had spent half the day going around to places on the West Side that said HOTEL and getting laughed at by the people sitting behind the reception desk for thinking they rented rooms by the night.

He closed his eyes for just a second, so he could concentrate better, but he must have dozed off, because when he opened them again, there was no one talking. Instead, while he watched in horror, the door to the *izba* opened, and his parents stepped out onto the roof, shushing each other. He started to get up, to explain everything, but then remembered he was naked, and when he went to cover his penis with his hand, he noticed that there were two of them, both terrifically erect. Why he'd never noticed this interesting fact before, he couldn't say. It made perfect sense: You have two eyes, two nostrils, two of just about everything else. He lay very still, using both hands to preserve his modesty, but when a big spider started crawling on his mouth, he couldn't resist brushing it away. . . .

Phoebe's big face was suspended over his, her hair hanging all around, tickling him. He lifted his head like a cat. The door was shut tight. One penis.

"What time is it?" he said, licking his lips.

"Shh," she said, planting damp kisses all over his face and neck. "Go back to sleep so I can watch you some more."

But he had to take a leak. It's probably a good thing we have bladders—otherwise who would ever get out of his nice warm nest? He went in the corner where there was a drain (*not* over the side of the building, as she proposed). Needless to say, she wanted to watch, she wanted to aim for him. But when it was her turn, she made him stand by the door with his back to her, and even then, even after he'd sworn on a stack of Bibles he would never, never peek, she ran behind some chimney pots and ducked down.

■

In the morning they breakfasted at Tom's, then took the subway to Columbus Circle. It was rush hour. Tim had woken up in an excellent mood. He kept thinking, I, Timur Borisovich Vorobyov, actually had sexual intercourse with an American girl. Her name is Phoebe Sayornis, and there she is!

The funny thing is, he felt like doing it again.

He put his mouth to her ear and said, *"Ya khochoo tebya."*

She looked at him, then put her ear back for more.

But instead of translating, he said, "Did you ever wonder what would happen if you jumped up in a moving vehicle? Like in a train or a boat. I mean, in the short time you were up, would the floor move slightly under you? Even a millimeter? Or, because you're in the train's atmosphere, would you land in exactly the same place?"

Slowly she shook her head.

"What?" he asked, offering *his* ear.

"No, I never wondered that."

He pretended to be shocked. "Aren't you interested in the laws of physics?"

She didn't say anything, just began jumping, but the conditions were all wrong for conducting a controlled experiment. Other passengers began nonchalantly moving away.

At Columbus Circle they chased each other out onto the platform, up the escalator that of course wasn't working, outside to where it was a sunny day. They walked along

59th Street, taking their time, every once in a while crashing into each other, until a block away from her hotel she stopped. She grabbed the tops of his jeans. "Don't go until the big hand gets to twelve. That's a long time from now." When the big hand did inevitably get to twelve, she said, "Don't go till it gets to one."

It was okay with him. He had literally nothing in the world better to do. The rest of the day stretched before him like the subway ride to Far Rockaway in Queens, where he used to go to the beach. He let her kiss his face with her suction-cup mouth.

It might be just mitosis, he was speculating: the cell that has divided remembering the good old days when it used to be one. And that's what rock 'n roll was all about.

Her hands that held his hands felt clammy, not like the girl's he dreamed of when she was still in Italy. Still, he would have gladly gone up to her room with her, on the off chance her mom wasn't there, but she shook her head.

After a while he began thinking that maybe they should just say good-bye and get it over with, but instead, *without* saying "good-bye," she spun around and began running— ran with all her might to the 59th Street entrance to the Plaza Hotel. The door opened and closed again.

She was gone.

He stood there, in other people's way, for several minutes, before turning around and heading home.

■

After Phoebe and her mom left for Knoxville, Tim went back to painting the house. It was a bigger job than he had expected. He had to stand on a ladder all day in the hot sun, scraping off the old paint and then rubbing with sandpaper until his hands told him that there were no more rough spots, but at least he could listen to the radio and think his own private thoughts. In the end the paint went on surprisingly clean and smooth. Neighbors out walking their dogs stopped to say how nice it was starting to look. They could hardly recognize the place, they said. Since he knew better than anyone else how it had looked before, he couldn't decide whether the paint was just a cover-up or new life.

It was still just Boris and him at home. In the evening they took their suppers outdoors. Boris had rigged a light in the peach tree so they could sit back there, taking turns reading aloud from a Turgenev novel—*Fathers and Children*. Once, as a Christmas present for his father, Tim had tried to read a Russian novel in Russian, but he had made it only to page 147. But reading out loud with his father was actually pretty fun. Tim's Russian was still fluent, though inevitably there were words he didn't know. Also, according to Boris, he had "ackvired" a slight American accent.

Boris pretended to be shocked and horrified.

One evening, when they had set the book down on the grass and were just sitting there, Tim mentioned that he liked a girl at school. His father listened. He said, in Russian, "It would be a pleasure to make her acquaintance."

Tim sighed. "I wish. She lives in another state."

They sat for a long time without talking, like two old bachelors.

His father would never have admitted how much he missed Yeva, but when she finally came home, on August 16, just in time for Tim's sixteenth birthday, he left for JFK two and half hours early.

She brought many presents, wrapped in layers of tissue paper. They were from friends and relatives to friends and relatives—every Russian who goes back for a visit must carry at least one whole suitcase for such presents.

She also brought *Baboolia*.

Now they could have the *novoselye*—it's an old Russian custom. All your friends come to see what a *beau-ti-ful* house you got, Boris! Incidentally, how much? Everyone had to go on a tour of the house, including all bathrooms and the basement.

Their guests came in two groups, first the Americans— the first friends they made in this country—and then, the next day, the Russians. To the Americans Boris kept bragging, "Tim is a pupil at a boarding school in New Hampshire."

"Oh yes, which one?"

"Aviary Prep."

"Aviary Prep?" They took another look at him, like maybe there was something about him they hadn't noticed the first time. He liked it that people were impressed, but it wasn't him, it was the school. It was as if the name AVIARY PREP was all lit up in neon letters, whereas *tim* and *boyd* were just words on the page.

He was the only kid his age. He wandered around the barely furnished rooms, picking cashews out of the nut dishes. A couple of people said, "So, Tim, where you planning to go to college? Harvard? Princeton? Yale?"

"I'm thinking of Brant," he said, enjoying the look of horror on their faces as they backed away.

For the Russian party everybody sat at one long table—it was really several tables pushed together. They ate and talked at the same time. Everybody clamored for news from the old country. They bombarded Yeva with questions. But there wasn't much news. People in Moscow were mostly living where they had lived all their lives, working at the same jobs.

Someone said that such inertia must be the result of seventy years of Communism. Someone else said, No, it was simply a characteristic of the Russian people. Tim had to go to the store to get more Coca-Cola. When he was coming up the walk, half an hour later, he could tell from the raised voices, spilling from the brightly lit house, that they were still at it.

He wondered if Americans had discussions like this.

So often when they were trying to cope in English his parents and their friends seemed comical. But what do you expect? Think how you would come across if you moved to a country where you didn't speak the language that well. Tonight, however, talking animatedly in Russian, they were all transformed before Tim's eyes into real people.

Sometimes he felt like joining in the conversation, but the truth is that he wasn't used to saying anything very complicated in Russian, and he didn't want to sound dumb in front of his parents' friends.

After dessert—by then it was ten o'clock—Tanya Yeroshkina went to the piano and played pieces by Chopin and Tchaikovsky. Olya Shulgina sang songs by Rachmaninoff. Then little Natasha, Olya's daughter—who had been grinning at Tim all evening, every time he would look at her—began playing jazz, and Boris and Yeva, followed by all their guests, got up to dance. His parents danced cheek-to-cheek like high-school sweethearts. (In fact, they met at university.)

Oh, and every few minutes, someone would proclaim, "I have a toast," and everyone would stop what they were doing to lift their glasses. They toasted friends still in Moscow, world peace, the New York Yankees—the party grew sillier and sadder. Someone started reciting a poem by Anna Akhmatova. Everyone, even Tim, joined in. They all knew it by heart.

Then they began singing songs about mother Russia.

Tim toasted with Coke. He was there in body, but his thoughts were with Phoebe, which made him feel like a spy.

Baboolia was sitting hunched over in an armchair. She hit him with her walking stick. "Who's the party for?" she asked in Russian.

"For our new house," he tried to explain. "We live in America now."

She looked at him with crafty eyes. "Who are you?"

Sometimes, to be honest, he thought she was a drooling idiot, but other times he wondered if maybe she knew something the rest of them didn't.

■

He wrote Phoebe two long letters, one in prose and one in verse, but all he got from her was a postcard which she had mailed in Italy. It had a picture of the Colosseum on the back and said, "Dear St. Timothy, How are you, I'm fine, and any other clichés you can think of. I'm getting tired of hanging around in bars while my mom goes off with Count Dracula. Wish you were here. Yellow blue bus."

He knew it was just a play on words, but when he repeated it out loud, his heart jumped.

Fall

She walked up to him in the parking lot, when the last bus from Logan Airport had finally pulled in next to all the parked cars. "Hi, lover," she said, and Frenched him right in front of Ms. Killdeer, the girls' lacrosse coach, and all the kids who were waiting for the driver to drag their junk out of the bowels of the Don't Take Us For Granite State Express. He had to take a step backward.

It's probably not a nice thing to say, but sometimes he couldn't help thinking that in Phoebe's pretty head where her brains were supposed to be there was a forest with birds twittering and leaves rustling in the breeze.

"Hi," he said, looking at her with a question mark.

She looked punk—cute punk. Later when he asked her why she had gotten so much of her hair chopped off on one side, she said that she used to be a tomboy, but now she wanted to change her image. This was sort of an in-between stage. "When I go to college, I'm going to be a woman," she stated. "But I don't want to, like, change over night."

She kissed him again, and somebody laughed.

They would have to hurry, Ms. Killdeer said in a voice that carried, if they were going to schlep all their stuff to their rooms and make it to the dining hall before it closed.

"So?" whispered Phoebe, and put her tongue in his ear. At first it felt weird; then he got an erection. She was hugging his one arm with both of hers. "Who cares," she said, "right?"

He dropped his suitcase and his dufflebag off in the Common Room of the Rookery. Then he had to go and check in with Doc Whimbrel, who put on his glasses to find his name on the list.

"*Kak proshlo vashe lyeto, Timofey?*"

"My summer was okay, sir. Yours?"

"Hot." Thin smile. "Well, back to reality," said Doc Whimbrel, taking his glasses off again.

Outside it was getting dark. Phoebe pushed off from the side of the building and gave him her hand—in public he liked it better when they just held hands. As they walked across campus, other kids running past in the semidark shouted, "Hi" and "How was your summer?"

"The best!" she called out, looking only at him.

He found he had two voices, one where your voice usually is and the other in the front of his pants. It turned out he was a born ventriloquist. The big dummy opened his mouth, and the voice from below said: "You want to, like, go somewhere?"

She didn't say anything, she just put her arm through his and shivered. She was grinning with her mouth slightly open.

They were really just walking, but it felt more like they were skimming over the playing fields where there were still little groups of fledglings with their parents, looking lost. You could tell they were new kids because they were all dressed up. It took a while to master the intricacies of Aviary's dress code, especially for those who had not grown up in the right kind of family (rich, American). Tim's first semester he naively wore jeans to the annual back-to-school *pique-nique*. All the other guys had on their jackets and ties. The French should have tipped him off, but what the *phoque*, he thought at the time.

Some of the parents looked like they weren't in such a hurry to leave, especially not after seeing this couple joined together like two octopuses, hurrying in the direction of the woods. They were probably having last-minute doubts about leaving young Willet or Polly there, far away from parental supervision.

As soon as Tim and Phoebe crossed the little concrete bridge, they stopped to say hello properly. Phoebe leaned away to take a good look at him, then started feeling his face and his chest, like a blind person. It was as if she wanted to be sure she wasn't just imagining things. When you're in love, sometimes it seems too good to be true.

And right when a force larger than them was pushing them into the woods, the silhouette of the last person he wanted to even think about emerged from the sunset.

"Chris," he said, by way of greeting.

Chris ignored him, as usual. "Phoebe Jane Sayornis," he rasped, not breaking his stride. "Born a Libra on the cusp of Scorpio in 1977, in Manhattan. Went to The Nestling School on Park Avenue, grades one through three. Parents divorced in 1985. Moved with mother to Knoxville, Tennessee, where she attended High-in-the-Branches Academy for Girls. Impressive verbal scores; so-so quantitative. Wants to be a doctor when she grows up—'So I can help people.' "

Phoebe was still anchored to Tim's arm, but she swung away and called out after him, "How do you know that stuff?"

"Because I care," said Chris, who was by then one long shadow across the playing fields.

"Because his mom works in the admissions office," Tim said. "He probably read your confidential file. We should report him."

She didn't say anything, she just hugged him tighter.

"I didn't know your middle name was Jane."

They should have known that the beaten path where students and faculty alike were supposed to run the Daily Mile would be like Grand Central Station during rush hour. Next came Snipe-Do, in AP running shorts that were about two sizes too big for her. She didn't stop, either—she just said, "Hi, kids," between huffs and puffs, and kept on going.

Still, he felt funny, since it had to be pretty obvious what they were up to. "Not here," he said, leading her off the strait and narrow, into the proverbial brier patch. It's a good thing he happened to have protection in his pocket.

■

What did it look like to have two juniors go into the woods and thrash around in there like a couple of bears and then be more or less quiet for ten or fifteen minutes? And then, when night had pretty much closed up the universe, come climbing back out, more subdued, all covered with *kolyuch-kas*—those little seeds that stick to your pants—and muck? Also mosquito bites where you would least expect to get them?

He wondered if there could be some innocent explanation.

We were just doing trust exercises, sir, for Outdoor Fitness. I thought from the way her teeth were chattering she might have hypothermia, so I was warming her up the fastest way I knew how. Neither of us could catch our breath, so we had to give each other artificial respiration (mouth to mouth).

If *he* had seen them groping back to the trail, *he* immediately would have assumed—so it must mean other people did, too. *Gospodi!* they were probably thinking. What's the world coming to?

It looked bad—he would be the first to admit it—but nobody else could know what it felt like at the time: What the cold leaves that had probably been on the ground since last fall smelled like (like graves), or the sinking sensation of muck being released from what he thought was solid ground and oozing into his brand-new corduroy pants from Eddie Bauer and his green J. Crew sweater made of 100% cotton ramie, or the hard stones that had probably been lying there since time immemorial. Nobody else could know what it felt like to have her watching him the whole time in the semidark, not quite smiling, but with her mouth slighly open, so you could see her will-o'-the-wisp teeth, her arms tight around him, hugging him, hugging him.

He kept thinking, my penis is in Phoebe Sayornis's vagina, as if without the official words his brain couldn't take in what his senses were telling him.

They walked back across the playing fields like Adam and Eve *after*. School was up on the hill, all lit up. It felt strange to be back—then he blinked, and it was all so familiar it was B O R I N G.

Phoebe dragged her feet. She kept making him stop and kiss her, and those kisses—so many, all over, like sudden raindrops before a thunderstorm—he didn't understand them then and he doesn't understand them now.

■

To have a girlfriend at boarding school—that was pretty amazing. Think about it. Acres of woods all around. No parents to offer their opinion. The school didn't exactly encourage such relationships, but there were no rules against them per se. The faculty had discussed once making sexual intercourse between students a major offense (i.e., one you could be kicked out for), but decided it would be too kinky to try to enforce. What were they going to do, make the boys eat uranium so they could trace their sperm with a Geiger counter? Put chirping car alarms in all the girls' underwear?

All the official rule book said was you couldn't be in the room of a member of the opposite sex, unless there was a faculty member on duty, and then you had to keep the door open at least six inches and have at least three of your collective feet on the floor.

Who wanted to go to somebody else's room, unless it was raining out? If it was raining out, they discovered this room in the Old Gym where they stored the mats for modern dance. You had to crawl in through the air vent. It was hot and sticky in there, but at least it was private. She had all the time in the world to teach him what to do for her, though sometimes his wrist got tired.

If it was nice out, Timur the spy preferred the woods, where you could hear someone coming for miles around. Phoebe, on the other hand, preferred to live dangerously. She liked to go someplace where there *were* people nearby— for example, up on the library roof. To get there without setting off the alarm, you had to squeeze through a window in the girls' bathroom and use the fire escape.

Once—this is a true story—they did it in a classroom under one of the big seminar tables. And who do you think should step into her room to get something? Yes, you are right, Snipe-Do. And if she had stooped over to see what those strange noises were of somebody being smothered to keep from laughing, she probably would have had a heart attack.

Even with dust in her hair and her pants peeled down, Phoebe looked beautiful.

Now they could be trial members of the Sex Club, if they wished, since they had made love on or under a seminar table. To become offical members—which Tim was in no hurry to do—you had to do it with someone you weren't going out with at the time. Phoebe said, "It would only be going through the motions. Think how cool it would be afterward!" There were rumored to be thirty-seven official members, known only to each other. He wondered about the fact that it was an odd number. But all he said at the time was, "You're crazy, you know it?"

Once Snipe-Do had left, they had the place to themselves. It was a powerful feeling—to be lying together at the center of the universe. Or, rather, the center of *this* universe: Aviary Prep. Tim lay on his back, a dictionary under his head. Phoebe lay with her head on his stomach.

"Talk to me," he said.

She lifted her head to look at him. "About what?"

"I don't care. About anything. About God. Or school. Or what you want to be some day. A doctor, right? You would make a great doctor."

"Yeah, I don't know anymore. It's hard to think of being just one thing."

"So be a doctor and something else. Anton Chekhov was both a doctor and a writer."

"Yeah, but that was a long time ago. Nowadays you have to be cutthroat just to get into medical school, and then you have to be a specialist, if you want to be really successful. My grandfather in Tennessee specializes in the gallbladder. He's made a fortune removing people's gallbladders. You should see the house he lives in, with big white columns. It's where my mom grew up. She says, 'This is the house that was built on the small pear-shaped organ that receives the bile.' "

She squirmed around to get comfortable. "Personally,"

she went on, "I don't know if I could devote my whole life to a single organ. I don't even know where the gallbladder is." She started probing her own tummy.

"You don't have to do anything you don't want to," he said, kissing her face, which was suddenly sharing Noah Webster with his. "What gives you the most pleasure?"

Her eyes opened wide; the tip of her tongue poked out of her mouth.

"Besides that."

"When I was a kid, I liked to finger-paint. I mean, all kids finger-paint, but I was, like, really into it. I loved it. Have you ever tried? Something about how close you feel to the medium. No brush, no nothing. But my mom would have a fit because I always got paint all over everything."

The clock ticked for several seconds.

"What do you want to be?"

"The first poet in space."

"Well, that's a good plan because you're halfway there."

Before they crawled back out from the dark space where on weekdays legs swung and crossed nervously, Phoebe solemnly wrote their names and the date next to all the petrified chewing gum and other mysterious stalactites hanging there.

I CAME TWICE! she wrote.

But afterward, when they were going back out into the sunny fall afternoon, they practically collided with Mr. Grouse, Dean of Students.

"Wait a minute," he blurted. "What were you kids doing in there?"

The dean's head looked like one of the totems on a totem pole. He glared at them through his wooden features. Tim couldn't think of anything to say, but Phoebe said in an angry voice, "Why? We weren't doing anything wrong."

"You're not supposed to be in there when classes aren't in session. These doors are supposed to be locked."

Phoebe shrugged, like it was his problem.

Afterward, Tim expected something bad to happen; she just thought it was funny.

She kept trying to get him to put a ring on her, but he couldn't stand the thought of sticking a needle in a place that was perfect as it was.

She also kept trying to get him to help her smoke the free samples of *marikhuana* that Chris Kite left in her p.o. box. They knew it was him because of the notes they came wrapped in. One said, "I want to touch your pain." He probably wants to touch your something else, Tim thought to himself, but he didn't want to put ideas in her head.

Chris had already graduated, but he had only gotten into two of the colleges he applied to, and they must not have been the right ones because his mom went around trying to find out who the traitor was among her colleagues on the faculty who could have written anything negative about her angel. Meanwhile, he was doing a postgraduate, or PG, year at AP so he could reapply to the right schools. He was taking courses like Anthropology and The Beat Poets, where you got a B just for showing up. He also had a job—all PG students were supposed to do some kind of work. Chris's job was to sell dope from a shack in the woods, on the bank of the river. Officially, he was in charge of the school's precious canoes and would insult you if you brought them back with even one little scratch on them.

"Just take one puff," Phoebe said, even though she knew

he was antidrug. "Well, just smoke me, then," she said, her rosebud lips coming up to his.

■

Mr. Grosbeak was their English teacher that year. He was so ugly, he was handsome—or, at least, that's what Phoebe said. He had an obscene proboscis.

"I bet he has a big one," she said once, smiling so you could see her two front teeth.

"Sick," Tim had said at the time, trying to look hurt.

"I'm just trying to explain something from a girl's point of view," she said. "I don't, like, have a crush on him. Now Dr. Godwit . . ."

Dr. Godwit was the school psychologist.

"You're perverted," Tim said. "He's at least thirty, and besides, he's married."

"So?"

"Girls are sick."

"Women," Phoebe corrected, looking about twelve.

"You're a turnip," he replied wittily.

Obviously this was *before* Mr. Grosbeak had stood up in chapel one day and told everybody he was gay. For the first time in the history of AP, probably, the old stone church got so quiet it must have sounded like it was summer and all the kids had left for vacation. Afterward, everybody was talking at once. Half the kids were like, Ooh, gross! But Tim and Phoebe decided it was really cool to be able to be honest about something like that. "I wish I was a lesbian," Phoebe stated at the time. "Then I could go around telling people."

In Mr. Grosbeak's class you couldn't just tear poems apart. You had to act them out. Everybody had to do a speech or a sonnet by the Bard of Avon, William Shakespeare. And you couldn't just say it, either—you had to communicate the feelings. You had to try and imagine that you were the person who was doing the talking.

Phoebe did Emilia's speech from *Othello, the Moor of Venice*.

> "But I do think it is their husbands' faults
> If wives do fall," etc.

It's a good play. If you've never read it, you should. Emilia is Iago the bad guy's wife, and she is saying that if men are going to fool around, women should be able to, too. According to Phoebe, Emilia is the only female character in the play who is even half believable.

Tim heard her say her lines so often that he learned them without trying. In class she was the only one who got it right the first time. She said the first part in a southern accent like her mom's; then, in a sort of parody of her own voice, she added Desdemona's comment at the end:

> "Good night, good night. God me such usage mend,
> Not to pick bad from bad, but by bad mend!"

It made his eyes water to hear her.

Personally he picked Sonnet 29, the one where Shakespeare is talking about being "in disgrace with fortune and men's eyes." It killed him that Shakespeare—*Shakespeare*—could feel this way, too. Unfortunately Tim is not a born actor, and Grosbeak kept stopping him and saying, "Not enough is getting through. We don't feel anything. How do *you* feel?"

It's not that Timur doesn't have feelings—it's just that he doesn't like going around expressing them all the time.

"Pay attention to the words," said Grosbeak. " 'Eyes?' "

Everyone's eyes were looking at Tim. "When people are looking at you funny?" he said. "Like you've done something wrong? Like you're a filthy pig?"

"Then shouldn't we be able to hear that?"

> "When in disgrace with fortune and men's eyes,
>   I all alone beweep my outcast state."

But it still wasn't right, maybe because he didn't really know what 'disgrace' meant.

"Help him, somebody."

"The opposite of 'grace'?"

" 'God shed His grace on thee.' "

When he got to the third quatrain, he happened to look at Phoebe.

> "Yet in these thoughts myself almost despising,
>   Haply I think on thee—and then my state,
>   Like to the lark at break of day arising
>   From sullen earth, sings hymns at heaven's gate;
>   For thy sweet love remembered such wealth brings
>   That then I scorn to change my state with kings."

For maybe ten seconds nobody said a word. Phoebe was grinning so hard she had knobs on her cheeks. Then Mr. Grosbeak went, "Phew," and everybody clapped.

That was probably the zenith. The zenith goeth before the nadir.

■

On a warm, still night they went swimming in Webber's Pond. A few stars floated on the dark water. Needless to say, they were both completely naked. As long as Tim lay near the surface, the water felt warmer than the air, almost. In fact, for some reason it seemed *better* than air, even though human beings can't absorb the oxygen in H$_2$O. But paddling around in this pond water was like bathing in a medium that both touched you and let you go. Maybe this was what it was like to be a fetus, he thought. Or a cosmonaut.

He was also, frankly speaking, very aware of his penis, which was as hard as a bone, even though, from the physiological standpoint, there's no bone there, just spongelike tissue which becomes turgid when the blood streams in (*Smart Sex*, page 29).

Neither of them said a word. They also didn't take their eyes off each other. When he swam over to lick her wet face, he couldn't help coming a little. She put her arms around his neck, like she wanted to dance—and they both went under. He couldn't breathe, they were sinking, he struggled violently to push her away. She somersaulted in the water. At first her white butt glowed like a rare fish. Then she sank deeper, out of sight.

On the pond's surface, the only sound besides the gently lapping water was the *who*? of an owl whose shadow flitted by.

"Phoebe?" he said in his normal voice, looking all around.

He did everything he had learned in Junior Lifesaving. He stayed calm, he inhaled until his lungs hurt, he dove down. A trail of bubbles rose past him. Far below some pale form shimmered, the heel of her foot, maybe, or the undulating body of a dead child.

If I breathe in, I will die, too, he thought, not unreasonably. Then he thought, Wait a minute, Webber's Pond was filled in years ago. Now it's a bank parking lot.

"Help!" he said in a strangled voice, as everything around him turned to cement.

He awoke to find himself in his bed at school—where

else? The sheets were slightly damp (*not* pee). His heart was beating so loud, Freddy would probably have heard it, if he hadn't been snoring like a bear.

Tim knew his dream was trying to tell him something. He knew what, too.

I'm going to have to have a talk with her, he decided, rehearsing until dawn what he would say.

Phoebe, I love you more than any other human being, more than I dreamed was possible, but what if we were, like, boyfriend and girlfriend on just Wednesdays and week-ends—that way, on other days I would be so looking forward to being with you?

Do it today! a voice said.

But that afternoon, just as he was clearing his throat, she said, "Tim, why do you love me so much?"

"Why?" he echoed.

They were standing by the river, looking out over the still water running deep.

"Because you're so unpredictable. I never know what you're going to say."

She looked at him eagerly, so he cudgeled his brains.

"Because you're so pretty. So smart. So crazy."

Her eyes had dropped a few millimeters, like she learning his words by heart, storing them up for another day.

He didn't know if he should say it or not, but did anyway: "Because I think you need me. Nobody's ever needed me before."

Her eyes were back on his, her look mischievous. "Think so, huh?"

"In fact, I love you more than any other human being, more—"

But she had had enough. She shut him up with kisses.

■

During the long hour before they opened the doors to the dining hall, Tim was jogging back from a hard run in the country. He was dressed in shorts and a sweatshirt. All you had to do was run due west from Webber's Pond for about fifteen minutes, and suddenly the evening smelled of cows and dry hay. He had been thinking his thoughts, enjoying his solitude, but when he ran through the parking lot of the Stop & Shop, there was Julie Crake (fate?), leaning up against somebody's car. She was wearing sweats and drinking a can of Diet Coke.

Over the summer Julie had gone to a fat kids' camp, and nobody could believe how much weight she had lost or how pretty she turned out to be underneath.

Tim ran circles in front of her, before slowing to a stop. "Julie," he managed to say, his hands on his thighs.

One of her orange eyebrows rose in a little arc. "Wow," she said. "I can't believe my senses. Romeo actually deigned to speak to me. This must be my lucky day."

He was still trying to catch his breath. "You headed back?" he said.

"Wait, you mean I can walk with you?"

"Quit it."

"Sorry," she said, shoving off from the car.

The houses on this side of town were all white clapboard with neat little fenced-in yards, not fancy like in the neighborhoods closer to the school. But walking along these streets you could imagine that Webber's Pond was a real town, where real families might actually choose to live.

After a minute Julie said, "Tim, we're friends, right?"

Oh, shit, he thought, but he looked at her and nodded. "Sure."

"Well, I just feel I should, like, warn you."

"Warn me?"

"Phoebe's my friend, too. I like her. It's just that—well, she acts one way in front of boys, in front of you, and another when she's in our house."

"Probably everybody does," Tim said.

"I don't want to say anything bad about her," Julie said.

"But?"

"Well, like she's always borrowing things and never giving them back."

Tim laughed out loud.

"And also she gets into fights with everybody, even her supposed friends. Have you ever seen her around Ms. Killdeer? Phoebe can be so hateful sometimes, and Ms. Killdeer's really nice—for a teacher."

Before Tim could say anything, Julie added, "She told me once I was fat. Well, I used to be fat, but none of my other friends ever said so. To my face, I mean."

Frankly none of this seemed that bad to Tim, but he just listened.

"She sneaks out at night—did you know that? I think to smoke dope, because she's crazy when she comes back."

Now Tim looked at her. They had stopped in the little triangular park that had the statue of a dying Union soldier, being mourned by a broad-lapped woman. Both were covered with pigeon shit. A bronze sign said in letters that were dripping green that this monument had been erected by subscriptions from patriots in the year of our Lord 1872.

"We always cover for her, but we're, like, worried." She looked solemn. "We're worried about you, too."

"Who's 'we'?"

Julie's face blushed orange. A smile flickered on her lips. "Mostly me."

"Well, thanks, I guess. I mean, I appreciate your concern, but I don't think you need to worry, okay?"

"You don't think she's using you?"

Tim laughed a short laugh. " 'Using'?" He felt his face and shoulders shrug. "Sure, in the good sense of the word. It's really our business, though, if you don't mind my saying so."

"Sorry."

They watched some pigeons pecking in the patchy grass. It's funny how all over the world where there are monuments, there are also pigeons, too. Reality principle.

"You don't have to be sorry," Tim said softly, because there were tear beads forming in the corners of Julie's eyes. She found a Kleenex in the kangaroo pouch of her sweatshirt and blew her freckled nose.

"I actually feel sorry for her," Julie said, smiling a crooked smile. "I'm not just saying that as a put-down. Her parents are awful—have you met them?"

"They seem pretty preoccupied with their own lives."

"Are you kidding? They're the most selfish, unloving people I've ever met. I mean, it's a miracle she's not crazier than she is. I don't think anybody's ever really loved her."

"I love her," Tim said. It sounded weird to be saying this, especially to Julie. It was like saying he believed in God.

Julie looked hard at him, almost like she was angry. "You can't save her, you know," she said calmly. "You can't save people from themselves."

"*I'm not trying to save her!* Besides, I think maybe you're exaggerating. Americans think everybody is crazy. Or—what's the word?—dysfunctional. Phoebe has her problems.

Who doesn't? By the way, what time is it? Shit, I have to go put on a jacket and tie. Aren't you coming to supper?" he added, because she had perched herself on the iron railing, which couldn't have been very comfortable.

Julie held up her Diet Coke, like she was toasting him. "Don't worry," she called after him, as he started to jog back to campus. "I also had a carrot and some cottage cheese."

■

That night at check-in Mr. Grosbeak said, "Tim, I'd like to talk to you." What is this, a conspiracy? Tim thought. He waited until after eleven, when no one else was around, then knocked on the door to his advisor's study.

"Come in." Big Nose was wearing *tapochki*—the things you wear on your feet when you're in your own home. "I made us some tea. We don't have to stand out here—come on into my living room."

In the living room, he said, "You know Mr. Woodcock?"

"Sure," said Tim. "Hi."

Mr. Woodcock placed a plate of brownies on the coffee table. "I'll leave you two alone," he said softly, going out.

For several seconds Mr. Grosbeak and Tim just sipped their tea in silence. Tim tried one of the brownies (delicious). Finally Mr. Grosbeak cleared his throat. "I won't beat around the bush, Tim. A lot of people are talking about you and Phoebe. You even came up in the faculty meeting today. So I felt I had to say something. You guys aren't being exactly discreet."

Tim knew that other people had to know, but when Mr. Grosbeak said so *officially*, it was like someone had shot a gun off in the room. The air started coming in waves. He wished he could act like he had an attitude and say "So?"—

but his mouth was full of brownie at the time. Also, his eyes—it often happens at inappropriate moments—began to water.

He can't even remember half of what Big Nose said, since it was the most embarrassing conversation he ever had in his whole life (even though his teacher did most of the talking), and he had retreated to where no words could reach him.

But then he realized his teacher had stopped talking. He was just staring at him. Perhaps he was smiling—it's hard to say, because this man was so ugly—except for his eyes, green and luminous, like a cat's, which looked deep inside Tim. In a husky voice the teacher was saying, "It may come as a surprise to you, but everybody has a sex life."

Tim felt hypnotized. He couldn't look away. And while their eyes were locked together, Mr. Grosbeak began telling him a story about when he was a kid, away at school, in love for the first time. It was hard to picture this old guy—maybe in his thirties or forties—pining away for another boy.

"Nobody has the right to get on his high horse and say what's right for you and me." The teacher sighed. "But we have to live in *this* world, where our behavior affects other people. Where people expect things of us. Want some more tea?"

"I have a lot of homework."

"Okay," Mr. Grosbeak said softly—suddenly it was as if the green eyes had released him, so he could look around the apartment for the way out.

At the door Mr. Grosbeak held out his big hand.

"May all of your wishes come clear, Tim,
    Whether or not they come true."

"It's from a poem," the English teacher said, smiling, when Tim looked at him blankly. "By Charles Pratt, one of my favorite poets."

Tim nodded, wondering if it was okay to stop shaking hands.

"You're a real person, Tim. That's more of a compliment than maybe you realize."

Probably he said the same thing to all kids in trouble, but Tim mumbled, "Thanks" anyway and got the hell out of there. For about two days he tried to hate that homo for sticking his gross beak into other people's affairs, then decided that maybe some day he would be a teacher.

■

It must have been a conspiracy, because at the exact same time Ms. Killdeer was having a chat with Phoebe. Unfortunately they got into a shouting match, and Phoebe said some things she probably wouldn't have if she hadn't been so upset. She said that Killdeer was a "hypocrite," since everyone in the house knew that she and Mr. Dowitcher humped each other every chance they got. She told the girls' lacrosse coach that all the girls in the house thought she was "pathetic."

He could have warned her what Phoebe was like when she got pissed at an adult. "I know it's hard for someone your age to understand these things," Ms. Killdeer said, with tears streaming down her face. "Bill and I love each other. He's getting a divorce, but it takes time."

They were sitting in the Common Room of her house when Phoebe told him her version of what had happened. She was still pretty upset. He tried rubbing her back, but it didn't seem to help. To tell the truth, he was kind of horrified at some of the things she had said.

"She's just doing her job. She's probably worried about you. Everybody has a sex life."

But he probably should have kept his opinions to himself, because she started giving him the evil eye.

"There, there," he said, patting her stiff back. The floor was littered with her used Kleenexes. Some girls started to come in, then quickly backed back out.

"Why don't they just leave us alone?" Phoebe wailed.

They went for a walk in the woods, then bought a package of sunflower seeds from a store downtown. Phoebe said that when she died she wanted to be buried with sunflower seeds in her hands, so she could come back as a flower. He decided just to humor her. He picked up some acorns from the sidewalk. "I want to come back as an oak tree," he stated.

At least she smiled.

He had a French test on *Le Petit Prince* in the morning, but some things are more important than tests and grades and getting into the college of your choice. Besides, according to Freddy Goatsucker, Madame Oiseau gave you at least a B if you said the Little Prince was a Christ figure.

They had arrived back at the river. Phoebe was stirring the dark water with a stick.

"Maybe we should, like, cool it," he heard his voice say. It was braver than the rest of him.

This was the hardest thing he had ever had to say. He had been thinking it for over a week and finally just blurted it.

She looked at him like she was going to spit.

"Not stop, just, like, not every day."

He went to put his hand on her arm, but she shook it off. "Fuck you." She threw her stick as far as she could, over the water. "I knew you'd betray me."

She swung around and started running back toward campus. He jogged the whole way, slightly behind her, trying to say he was sorry.

■

The whole top of her face looked sad, but she kept whacking the mirrors.

"What?" he said, because she kept looking at him out of the corner of her eye.

It was a few days after their quarrel—if that's the right word. Supposedly they had made up, but when he tried to kiss her, she twisted her face, so that instead of lips he got earlobe and hair. They were on the front porch of her house. He was just soaking up the sunshine, keeping her company while she worked on her project for the all-school art fair at Andover. Now that she was flunking math and chemistry and not likely to ever get into med school, her new goal in life was to be a famous sculptor. Then Goshawk would have to say, Honey, we underestimated you. (This is Tim being cynical.)

She'd bought about ten of those little rectangular mirrors they sell at Woolworth's, and now she was smashing them to smithereens with her big hammer. Later she was going to glue the pieces into a mosaic and entitle it "Reality?"

It was a Saturday, one of the days he was setting aside for her—for them. He had just called her up and said, "Can I come over?" and she had said, "Sure"—as in, Why wouldn't it be?

So here he was, trying to be patient, because he was feeling good. He had just gotten back a chemistry test, which he had only studied for for a couple of hours, and he got a 92 on it.

So maybe he had been worrying for nothing? Besides, he was in the mood.

She looked serious, banging away at her mirrors. Her hair on the long side kept getting into her eyes, and she kept brushing it back almost angrily.

"What?" he said again.

All he had asked was, "Do you want to go to the dance tonight?" There was a dance every Saturday night in the Old Gym. Sometimes they went, and sometimes they did something else.

But instead of saying what *she* wanted to do, she just kept breaking mirrors. Finally, she held the hammer in midair. "It's no big deal, but it's going to make you sad. And I don't want to make you sad. Probably mad, too," she added, whacking a mirror right in the center so that the cracks spread out in concentric circles and stayed that way, unlike in water.

It seemed incongruous that the day should be so balmy. In Russia they have a good expression for such a day: *bab'ye leyto*. It means a piece of the summer left over for old peasant women. He was already feeling sad and mad, even though he had no idea what she was talking about.

He said, "You *have* to tell me now. You don't like me anymore?"

"*No*, silly, of course I do. But in a way that's the problem: You're going to think I don't. But it has, like, nothing to do with us. We're still—what we are. That's what I want to tell you. It's hard to explain."

She looked at him and smiled, and he couldn't help smiling, too, but his face felt like one of her broken mirrors.

"You like someone else?"

Her look flew in his direction, but didn't quite land on him.

"Who is it?" he made himself say. "Ibrahim?"—because she told him once she thought Ibrahim, this kid from Detroit, was the handsomest kid in the school. But she turned to him with a dark and silent look and shook her head.

"Tim, it's nothing. I just feel I should tell you—that Christopher's taking me to the dance. He asked me, and I thought we had broken up so I said yes."

For a moment it looked like there was more coming, but she stopped there, gathered bits of broken mirror into a glittering pile, and sort of as an afterthought glanced at him for maybe the hundredth time.

He sat up, swallowing air like a fish. "Christopher?" he said. "As in Chris Kite?"

It felt as if someone had punched him in the solar plexus, and atoms and molecules—if, like God in heaven, they really exist—were orbiting around his head.

Or, rather, he was right where he had been, but it felt like he had gotten up and walked a long way off.

He wanted to say, "Why?" Ibrahim he could understand—he was a nice kid, he played Brahms on the piano. But Chris would be like going out with Count Dracula. Not for the first time in his life, it seemed like all the secrets of the world were behind locked doors. He was never going to understand relationships, so why even try?

"That's what *I* call him." She pretended to be looking for her hammer, but really she was watching him from under her eyebrows. "I told you you would be mad," she said in her spoiled brat voice.

"I don't mind if you go out," he heard himself say, calmly. "We're not, like, engaged. It's your business—I can't stop you. Maybe I'll ask Julie and see you there."

It's funny. He could write pages about Julie Crake, and maybe someday he will. But though he liked her a lot as a friend, he didn't feel any sparks. Whereas sometimes he didn't even like Phoebe, but he couldn't help loving her.

"Unless," he added, "you mean you want to break up?"

"*No*! No. That's what I don't mean."

"Well, you want to meet after the dance then?"

She shook her head, her face hidden now.

"I'm just trying to understand," he said, hugging his knees.

"I can't meet you afterward, not tonight—and, Tim, I really don't want to talk about this." Now, finally, she was staring at him, hard—or, more like squinting at him, her face pale: Now do you get it, you dumb Roosky?

"Phoebe, that guy—"

"Don't say it," she warned.

"You know, he uses people."

"Not me, he doesn't."

"He may hurt you."

She shouted, "DON'T, TRY, AND, PROTECT, ME!" Then, in a milder voice, she added, "I'm sorry, but I don't need advice from you of all people—even if you're right."

After a long pause he said, "I'm sorry, too."

She was staring at the ground in front of her. "You're making me all confused. I wish I had never said anything!" She sat there, her head slightly bowed, holding the hammer in her hand, then her chin started wagging and real tears fell. For a few seconds Tim wished they still loved each other because then he could put his arms around her and try to make her feel better.

■

He stood up, only at first his feet weren't where he had left them. "I have to go," he heard himself say in a voice that had no spit in it. He said, not going, "I have pain in my chest."

She stood up, too, carefully clapping mirror dust and

splinters off her hands, so she could use the backs of them to wipe her eyes. They were hands that just a few seconds ago he could have reached over and taken in his—only now they and the tear-smudged face and everything else about her was definitely *not his*. She was private property: POLICE TAKE NOTICE.

"Don't . . . tell . . . me . . . it's . . . no . . . big . . . deal," he said, panting.

She must have felt something like he did, because she took a step toward him, then stopped. It was funny—not ha ha funny—that only one week ago he was wishing for more breathing space, and now, like a fish jerked into the bright blue air, he was drowning in it.

She followed him out into the street. The front gate clicked shut. He turned around. She was standing with her private hands in her private pockets. His were in his pockets. They just happened to be standing in the street that leads to town—where he saw her at her window one night in December, less than a year ago.

First you're friends, then something happens—you're boyfriend and girlfriend—you can hardly believe it! And then you're strangers—except in your dreams, where the other person appears unchanged, probably because half the time your unconscious is still living in the past.

"I'm not . . ." she said, breathing, breathing (you could see her chest rise and fall).

Breathing, breathing, he looked at her.

". . . telling you it's no big deal. I don't know what it is. It's happening. That's all. I'm in the midst of it. I'm amazed I can like someone like that. I'm even more amazed he likes me back."

"Someone like what?"

"I know you don't like him, but you only see what he's like on the outside. Inside he's vulnerable and sweet. I feel honored that he . . . trusts me. I don't expect you to understand."

He couldn't help grinning, but it, too, was only on the outside. Inside, he was thinking evil thoughts. But she saw only the smile. She took her hand out of her pocket and experimentally touched his chest, approximately where his heart used to be, but it must have felt like wood or something, because she took her hand back again. She put it back in the pocket of her jeans.

Then some of the evil things he was thinking came spewing out. The grin was still there—it didn't matter, he liked the way it felt on his face. He said things on purpose to hurt her, watching while her face crumpled and she started to cry, this time not even taking her hands out of her pockets to brush away the tears.

Then he was walking in another part of campus, out across the playing fields. Somewhere in the middle of the woods he pulled himself up into a tree and quickly climbed from limb to limb to where the branches started swaying. He sat there until he had to take a leak, then pissed on the world below. Gradually it grew darker and darker, the first stars appeared, distant bells and kids' voices sounded like birdsong in the wind. Wrapping his own arms around himself couldn't keep out the cold. He craved a Big Mac with large fries, a vanilla shake, and a cherry pie.

Something made him think of Phoebe—for two hours he had been deliberately thinking of everything but. In his mind's eye he saw her still standing in the street, her shoulders slightly hunched. He thought, This is crazy, and climbed down from the tree.

■

The lights were on in the Old Gym. A band was still playing: mostly you could hear the beat. Tim walked up the ramp which was lined with chattering groups and a few quiet couples, poised for the eleven o'clock bells. "Hey, Tim," someone called, "where's Phoebe?"

He stood in the shadows behind the net, his hands in his back pockets. Only the usual dancers were out on the floor, the hard-core couples who liked to neck in public, standing up. There were also freshmen girls who flopped around like puppets, then ran screaming into each other's arms. A few guys in baseball caps tapped their feet to the music but didn't venture forth. For once the band wasn't bad.

He was back outside, heading toward the quad, when the bells starting ringing. Kids ran past, calling out last-minute messages. Happy kids, though probably they didn't know it. He walked by Whippoorwill House. Sarah Shrike was leaning over the porch, saying something to a kid on the street. She was shivering in her pale green sweater. In a second she would be inside where it was warm.

"Sarah, have you seen Phoebe?"

She looked at him—Is this a good guy or a bad guy now? "She had a date" was all she said.

"Is she back yet?"

She was still looking at him, the same way, sort of appraisingly. She slowly shook her head.

He had to knock on the door of his dorm to get inside. Luckily there wasn't a teacher or proctor standing in the hall. He just wandered into his dorm parents' apartment and crossed his name off the list. Chris's name was crossed off, too. That meant he should be in the dorm somewhere. However, Tim didn't see him.

■

He vaguely remembers Freddy coming into the room, briefly turning on the light. Some time around three or four in the morning, there was a sound like a gun being fired. He sat up in bed. Outside a steady rain was thumping on the fallen leaves. He got out of bed and put on his clothes.

He grabbed his poncho that folded up into the size of a wallet, which he had never used before, and when he was out in the empty hall, he opened it and put it on. It smelled like a condom. Downstairs, he pulled the thin hood over his head, then leaned against the bar of the main door and tumbled out into the night.

Or early morning. The sky was cloudy bright, in spite of the rain. The sleeping school looked peaceful. It didn't *feel* like he was doing anything wrong, though he understands why there is a rule against leaving your dorm before 6 A.M.

Her window was slightly open at the bottom. In his normal voice he said, "Phoebe?" Then he crossed to the sidewalk on the other side. When no shadowy face appeared, he tried tossing pebbles up against her screen.

He eased the front gate open and went up the walk. Someone had swept up the broken glass from the porch, but you could still see the glittering powder. The doorknob wouldn't turn.

Heading out to the playing fields and the woods beyond, he felt quite calm. He was in an experimental, let's-see-what-will-happen frame of mind. In fact, a wave of excitement seemed to lift him up. The rain felt good on his face. It wasn't falling that hard, but you could hear the noise it made in the grass, in the trees.

Just as he reached the canoe shack, the moon emerged from the clouds that were rushing past, silvering the river.

The door rattled when he knocked on it. He climbed up on a low boulder that some glacier had spent eons dragging there on its huge slug back.

Somebody said, "Shit. Can you see who it is? I bet it's Grouse."

"It's Tim," he said in a normal voice.

For a while everything was still, except for the sound of rain, which goes on oblivious to fortune and men's eyes. A minute passed, it felt like, then the door opened, and Chris stepped out, wearing only his pants. He made sure the door was closed behind him.

"What do you want, Roosky?"

"I want to talk to Phoebe. Is she in there?"

Chris looked at him. "If she is, it's because she wants to be, okay? I mean, I don't want to hurt your sensitive feelings or anything, but you don't, like, own her."

"Phoebe, can I talk to you for a second?"

Chris turned his head slightly, as if looking through a crack, then looked back, grinning. "She doesn't want to, okay? So why don't you beat it? I mean, if you guys were, like, spending the night in the woods, I wouldn't come barging in on you. You have a lot of nerve. Are all Rooskies as chauvinist as you?"

Inside the shack someone giggled and then moaned. He didn't stop to think about Human Values or talking things out. He swooped down. In the past he wouldn't have wanted to get so close to Chris, but the next thing anyone knew there were two boys rolling around on the hard ground, trying to wrestle and punch each other at the same time.

Maybe Chris looked like a bag of bones, but really he was more like Scylla, the sea-monster in *The Odyssey* that has six heads and twelve octopus legs. Timur was bigger and stronger, but just when he got his enemy's wrists pinned down, the head rose up to bite him. It could also spit upward.

The door to the canoe shack swung open, and Phoebe, wearing only a blanket, stepped out. "You guys," she said. She wandered around barefooted, like she was looking for somewhere dry to sit. "I don't feel so good."

"Go back inside," Chris grunted. "Just let me get this idiot off me, and I'll get you something. Get off me, you fucking idiot!"

It would be a lie to say Timur did not feel like murdering the boy lying under him, but instead he shook his wrists, then got up and went over to Phoebe. He drew the ends of her blanket together so that they covered her frontal nudity.

"Where are your clothes?"

"Where are my clothes?" she echoed. "I know I was wearing clothes."

He went in the shack to look for them. It was like a religious shrine in there. There were candles burning, also some kind of incense.

Chris was still sitting on the ground, his shoulders moving up and down with each breath. "Yeah, well, when this asshole leaves, I'll get them for you."

She kept shivering in spasms, her face a pitiful moon, round and pale. Tim went up to her and turned around. "Get on my back." When he felt her uncertain arms around him, he held her wrists and boosted her up. He had to buck two or three times to get her high enough. Then he said some Russian words to Chris that are too rude to repeat in English.

Chris was grinning in the dark. "You're going to carry her all the way back to campus like that? Be my guest. Jesus, what a dumb fuck."

★   ★   ★

He really and truly did search for one of the paths that led back to the playing fields, but a sort of fog rising from the ground made the going rough. She was not exactly light, and it didn't help that she kept choking him. He hadn't forgotten that he was mad at her and hurt—those were things to think about later. He danced her higher up his back, gripping her arms. Her legs held on, around his middle. She put her warm cheek against his.

A branch caught on his poncho and shook a shower on their heads. She jerked and shouted, "Quit it! Don't touch me!" He stooped, trying to see her over his shoulder. Since she was quiet again, he continued tramping in the direction of the pale sky ahead.

■

"Put me down."

"No. You don't have shoes."

"Yes, but I have to throw up."

He lowered her feet to the ground just in time. Putting her hands on her bare thighs, she vomited into the bracken, the blanket first coming open in front and then falling off her back.

She used the back of her hand to wipe her mouth. "Where are we?"

"I know where we are."

"Yeah? Well then, why have we been wandering around for hours it feels like? My head kills. What are you doing?"

He had pulled the poncho over his head and was taking off his shirt. "Here," he said, putting her arms into the sleeves, helping to button it up. It was a flannel shirt (extra large), which fit her like a minidress. "Put these on, too," he said, giving her his Jockey shorts. He still had his pants and T-shirt. "Keep the blanket, only—here—let's put my belt around it."

He backed against a tree trunk to catch his breath. Overhead, among the dripping branches, the sky was maybe clearing slightly.

"Tim, where are we?" She looked around, like someone just regaining consciousness. "What was that? It sounded like a truck."

"Come on." He pushed away from the tree trunk.

In another twenty meters they came to the edge of a highway. In fact, a big truck, an eighteen-wheeler, was laboring uphill past a Sunoco station. Beyond was a motel, its sign still glowing. Neither of them spoke. They walked along the edge of the road, like a couple of hitchhikers.

■

A kid who was maybe sixteen, wearing a poncho, sat on a metal chair under a small neon sign that said OFFICE. It was shortly after six. A cloud hovered over the parking lot and neat lawn. Out of nowhere a nondescript bird flew onto the pavement and took some practice hops. It was probably looking for a nice, juicy worm.

The door to Number 34 had been ajar for several seconds, and now a man in a business suit backed out, carrying two suitcases and, under his arm, a leather briefcase. He said something to whoever was still inside in an early morning voice. The door opened again and a young woman came out. She was dressed in nice clothes, like an executive secretary or a second wife.

"What should I do with this?" She dangled a key.

"Leave it on the bureau. Just pull the door behind you."

The kid rose from his metal chair. "Morning," he said, pushing back the hood of his parka.

The man shut the car trunk—it didn't make that much noise.

"You're from Massachusetts. We get a lot of people from Massachusetts up here. Everything okay? No problems? I can take the key."

The lady in the fancy clothes handed it to him, her eyes on the man, who straightened up. "No, no problems. Very comfortable, in fact. I've always wanted to try this chain." He took a fat wallet out of his back pocket, hesitated, then took out five bucks and gave it to the kid.

"Thank you!"

The boy touched the key to his forehead, as the car backed around and then pulled onto the highway. "Have a nice day!" he said softly. Then he unlocked the door to Number 34 and went inside. A few seconds later, a Native American with a blanket wrapped around her followed him.

"Look, they only used one bed. Go take a hot shower. I'll get us some candy bars and Cokes from the machine outside. Snickers okay?"

■

Through the cheap door he could hear her on the toilet, making noises all human beings make. *This* was probably what it meant to love someone: to accept all their noises. It was like a new test: Do you really love this difficult person? Could you go through life with her?

On "Today" they were showing pictures of people in the former Soviet Union standing in long lines. There was already snow on the ground. Old people on pensions gathered around the cute American reporter. They told her it hadn't been this bad since the war. Phoebe came out of the bathroom, naked as a young child, using a towel to dry her mass of tangled hair. She looked at the TV screen, then at Tim, and raised her eyebrows.

The drapes were shut, the air conditioner running. In America they have achieved such mastery over the environment that except for the occasional car starting, it could have been almost any time of day or night. Under the covers they snuggled against each other to get warm. She fell asleep in his arms. In retrospect it's a romantic picture, but it wasn't so comfortable at the time. His underneath arm was being squished.

She sighed once—a long breath in and out. Later she began fighting with the covers, finally kicking one foot free. He took advantage of the moment to get his arm back and sit up like a cat.

She looked like she was marching somewhere. Where?

He put his head back down on the pillow. His face was against her damp hair. He kissed the back of her head, where there were bumps which probably only he knew about.

And then he was standing on a hill of snow at the Danilov Monastery in Moscow, holding up a big snowball in his gloved hand, while someone took his picture. Or, rather, *he* was the one taking the picture, focusing on the ten-year-old boy in the giant fur hat, ear flaps flapping. At first he didn't recognize himself. "I want to remember the snow," the boy said solemnly in a high voice. "In case we move somewhere hot like Africa."

■

EAT HERE, a blinking sign suggested. It was pretty convenient: right next to the motel. The day was cold, no visible sky, just clouds. He had gone through his pockets, calculating to the last penny how much breakfast they could afford.

The sign said NO SHOES, NO SERVICE, but he had scooted into the booth and hidden his wet stocking feet under the bench long before the waitress arrived with her coffeepot. Maybe he *was* a little underdressed for fall—in just a T-shirt and jeans—but you know how crazy kids are nowadays. Phoebe pushed the hood back from her tangled hair, then pulled the poncho up and over her head. A fly on the overhead Tiffany lamp would probably have thought, what a nice plaid mini. Only a troll squatting under the table could see her boy's underwear and big shoes.

Apropos of nothing, he felt a surge of love for her.

To the waitress he said, reading from the menu printed on his place mat, "Two fresh eggs sunny side up, toast and jelly, sausage and hash browns, and orange juice, please."

"Ah, better let me see if we're still doing breakfast." Returning, she said, "You're just in time. Miss?"

Miss said, "Could I have hot chocolate, please? And blueberry pancakes? And a glass of orange juice?" She always ordered like that, in questions. Yes, darling, you can have all these things, plus a tip for the waitress, and there will still be $7.32 left over—to live on for the rest of our lives.

Later, wiping up egg with his last piece of toast, he looked up. "What?" he said, because she was smiling at him.

"Nothing. I like to watch you eat."

He put the toast in his mouth and patted it shut. "So now we have to plan, okay? Now what?"—because she was slowly shaking her head.

"You're crazy, that's all. You realize we're in deep doo-doo. How do you say doo-doo in Russian? If we're lucky, they'll put us on probation. They'll probably kick us out."

"Phoebe." He took a deep breath. "You know we're free now? We can go anywhere, literally. So, like, where do you wish to go? You want to know what I was thinking? Canada.

In a few hours we could be to the border. I looked at a map once. We keep going north, past Montreal, to where the roads stop—then what? That's where most of Canada is: past where the roads stop. Maybe we'll come to a small village with friendly aboriginal peoples. I'll get a job. We can both get jobs. In the evening we can read books, educate ourselves. Learn Mohawk, Ojibwah, all kinds of languages, in addition, of course, to French. Buy a snowmobile."

She was grinning at him.

"Have many babies?" she said, raising one eyebrow.

"Sure, why not? Two boys and two girls."

"Yeah, well," she said, looking down. "I'm not so sure I want kids."

"No rush. I want to write a book. You can make sculptures. I'm serious: whatever you want. If later we decide to go to college, we can."

"Have you, um, ever been to Canada? I won't even ask how we'd get there."

"Easy. Hitchhike."

"Listen, at the border, they ask you stuff like where you were born. If you say Moscow, they'll make us get out and go inside this little building. If you say *anything*, with your accent—"

"I don't have any accent."

"You don't have much of one, just certain words. It's cute and all, but still they'll, like, arrest us."

"So we don't have to cross where there are guards. We'll bushwhack our way across the border. They haven't got any barbed wire there. We'll go up to the first person we meet. *Bonjour, monsieur. Comment allez-vous?* Your French is better than mine. Tell him we're lost. *S'il vous plaît, monsieur, où est la route*—that goes north? How do you say that?"

"Then what?"

If somebody had seen them then, heads bowed over their mugs, maybe they would have felt like helping them make their getaway. Because his plans were out of the ordinary doesn't mean they wouldn't work.

Somebody *did* see them.

A waiter came up behind them—no, it was Dean Grouse in a trenchcoat. "You kids have any idea how much trouble you've caused us? We've got half the state out looking for you."

Phoebe clenched. For a couple of seconds it looked like she was going to make a run for it. Then she sat back and took a long swallow of her hot chocolate.

The lady dean—Ms. Swift—appeared around the man one. "Are you kids all right? I'll call Dunlin. Tell him we've found them. Will he be relieved!"

■

It was a revelation to look out the windows and see the bigger world beyond school. A mailman in a truck with right hand steering was sticking letters in mailboxes. In the sodden fields only stalks remained. At an unattended country food stand, amid bright pumpkins of different sizes, a scarecrow was sitting in a soggy heap. What was left of his face had a foolish smile.

Phoebe and Dean Grouse did most of the talking. Dean Swift drove.

"We were out jogging. We got lost."

"Dressed like that?" Grouse, sitting sideways, threw a look over the back of his seat.

Under the poncho Phoebe's legs looked bare and raw. She said, "You can believe me or not, it doesn't matter. It so happens that tomorrow is my killer day. I have a paper due and two tests. I got up early, went for a run, to relieve stress. It started to rain. We waited under some trees. We must have taken a wrong path somewhere. That's the honest-to-God truth."

He could only admire her. They had been caught red-handed, yet she seemed calm, confident. "We got up early to run the Daily Mile. We must have gotten lost. Just out of curiosity, is that against the rules?"

"Tim," said Ms. Swift, looking at him in the rearview mirror. "What happened to your face? It looks like your eyebrow's cut."

He put his hand to his face. There was dry blood. He smiled and shrugged.

Phoebe said, "So put us in jail, if you want to."

They stopped at a red light. Ahead were the all-too-familiar red brick buildings. Swift's eyes were in the rearview mirror. "Before you perjure yourselves, I better tell you there was a fire drill in your dorm last night, Tim." The light turned green, and she drove past the boat house on their right, around the bend to the Administration Building. "It was unscheduled. At first we thought someone must have pulled the alarm, as a prank, but that doesn't seem too likely, does it, at five o'clock in the morning? My guess is that some bug crawled into the smoke alarm; it's happened before. As of five this morning you weren't in your room. Doc Whimbrel checked. Your roommate said he had no idea where you were or when you left. He said you had seemed troubled lately. Your dorm parents contacted Security; they contacted us."

The car came to a stop in the curved driveway right by the front steps of the Administration Building. Once she had gotten the gear shift into park, Swift turned around in her seat to look at them. "We checked your room, too, Phoebe."

"That was at 5:26 A.M.," said Grouse, looking at the clipboard he held in his lap.

A picture appeared in Tim's mind. Ms. Killdeer, with her hair down like Lady Macbeth, unlocking the door to Phoebe's room. Girls in nightgowns, awakened by the commotion, behind her, trying to see in.

"So we think the best thing for everybody concerned would be for you simply to tell the truth."

■

When they got out of the car, he realized how strange they looked. He was covered with mud. His socks were soaking wet—he left footprints everywhere he went. Daylight revealed that under the poncho Phoebe was wearing only a shirt. Size extra large, but still. Between the hem of the poncho and a pair of boy's shoes, her legs were bare.

In other words she was lovelier than ever.

She was making faces at him, sort of scrunching her features and staring hard. He knew she was trying to convey some message by means of mental telepathy—but what was it? Would it be absolutely inappropriate to kiss her on the mouth? It's what he felt like doing.

"Go back to your house and take a shower," Swift told Phoebe. "Put some clothes on and meet us back here in an hour. Tim, are you able to answer some questions?"

"Go!" Grouse ordered, when she lingered, trying to send one final message to Timur by wiggling her eyebrows.

At last she walked away, across the quad.

"She used to be so sweet," Dean Swift said, as they stood there watching her. "When did she get to be such a rebel?"

Tim didn't know whether to glare at her or smile in sympathy. She's *farouche*, he felt like saying. His French teacher had explained that this word meant someone who is both "bold" and "shy" at the same time. Like an untamed creature.

In Soviet movies there was usually a good guy—a tough-on-the-outside, but underneath-heart-of-gold Soviet intelligence officer—being interrogated by tall, lanky, uptight CIA agents. They would stand in a circle like so many vultures, bombarding our hero with questions.

So it came as a surprise when Ms. Swift brought him some cheese and crackers and asked if he would like a cup of tea. While he was sitting there, leafing through the Sunday *Boston Globe*, his roommate showed up with a paper bag. In it were more or less clean socks and sneakers, and his hooded Harvard sweatshirt.

Then you said, Eumaios—O my swineherd[1]—"Good luck, pal," and hit him softly on the shoulder.

"Thanks," Timur muttered, looking up.

Then he was alone again, in a room that resembled a museum of early American furniture. From one of the walls, the school's founder, Reverend Crossbill Hatch, looked down at him. In this rather primitive painting, the Reverend Educator was holding a book—presumably the Bible—in one hand, and, in the other, a pitcher of water raised to his ear. Each year incoming students were taught the symbolism of the pitcher. Besides founding his school to educate American boys, Hatch went around the country, preaching hydropathy, or the taking of cold baths, as a cure for disease and impure thoughts.

Both deans came in, closing the double doors behind

[1]Homer, *The Odyssey*, p. 249.

them, and carried armchairs over to where Tim was sitting. They asked him only a couple of questions: What time had he left his dorm? Had he intended to run away?

Dean Swift briefly explained how the disciplinary system worked. First he should write a truthful account of everything that had happened. Then, if he wished, he could also write a personal statement, explaining any so-called extenuating circumstances.

"Excuse me?"

"Anything that will help the Disciplinary Committee understand your point of view."

The secretary appeared. "Tim's mother is on the phone," she said gently.

The deans looked at each other, then at Tim.

Grouse picked up the phone on the desk. "Hello?" He listened, nodding. "It's all right, Mrs. Boyd. They're fine. He's right here. Would you would like to talk to him? Just a minute, please."

"*Allo!*"

"Timka! Moy Timka! Boris Yeltsin. Oy, veh! *Nos, glaza,* rot—vodka. Yellow blue bus, Timka!"

"*Mama!*"

"Don't say anything about—you know—Chris, okay? They're going to try to keep us apart so we can't get our stories straight. Listen, do what you have to do. I'm personally going to deny everything. We met early to run the Mile. Killdeer was giving me shit just the other day, because I haven't run it in weeks. That's pretty ironic, huh? Are you okay?"

The deans had tiptoed out of the room to give him privacy.

He said, "You know he was probably the one who pulled the alarm."

"I know, I know. He's sick. But I did what I did of my

own free will. He didn't, like, force me. I guess you know
we smoked some heavy dope."

The deans were back again. *"Nyet, mama,"* Tim was
saying. *"Ne bespokoysya."*

"They're back, huh? Listen, what I was saying, if you have
to tell on him to save yourself, I'm not going to blame you.
He'll deny it, so it'll be your word against his. Just so you'll
know, he's more into drugs than sex. He does heroin, can
you believe it? He's very self-destructive. I'll be amazed if
he survives college. Shit," she said, "Madame Wench is
coming!" The phone went dead.

Tim said, *"Poka, Mama."*

"Don't hang up!" Grouse said. "If you're through, I'd like
a few words with her."

Tim held the receiver to his ear. "It's too late."

"Call her back."

He shrugged and dialed his own number in area code 718.

His dad's booming voice came on the line. "Allo! Glat
you telephoned. We can't come to the phone now, but eef
you will leave myessage after beep, we'll call back as soon
is possible." Then, as an afterthought, he added, "Have a
nice day!"

Tim turned slightly from the deans' hawk eyes and said,
in Russian, "It's me. Call as soon as you get home, okay?"

He was just about to hang up, when on the other end
there was a clattering sound, and then a voice was crying,
"Kto vy? Shto vy khotite?"—it means, Who is this and what
do you want?

"Baboolia. Granny, it's me, Timka." He was speaking
Russian, of course.

"Timka?" the old woman replied. "He's not here. Everyone says he has gone far away. Maybe he's in a camp or
dead, I don't know."

"No, it's me, Granny. I'm alive. I'm at school."

Grouse was standing next to him, his hand out, so Tim said in Russian, "Wait one second, Granny," and passed him the phone.

"Hello, Mrs. Boyd," said the dean, smiling his totem-pole smile. "We have a slight problem—what's that? I beg your pardon?" He covered the mouthpiece and whispered, "Doesn't she speak English?"

"Not when she's upset," Tim said. "Try German. People in her generation learned German."

"I don't speak German."

"Try French then. She speaks a little French."

"*Bonjour, Madame. Comment allez-vous?*" A look of panic flashed in his eyes. He said to Tim, "I studied French for four years, but I don't really speak it." Then he said, "She hung up!"

"It's okay. Don't worry so much. My dad will call when he gets home. You can talk to him."

■

The next few days—until Thursday, when the Disciplinary Committee met—went by in a haze, maze, daze (whichever is correct). Tim felt numb, or rather he felt like the real him had contracted down to the size of a parakeet; the big galoot with the baseball cap was just a decoy whose eyes he looked out of.

This feeling was intensified because no one *acted* like he was in trouble. No one said, "Shame on you, you hooligan." If they spoke to him at all, it was in polite, hushed voices.

He used one of the school's computers to write his "Account of What Happened." The jist of it was: "I left the dorm before hours and went to the woods. I couldn't sleep. My girlfriend and I had had a fight, and I needed time to think. I hadn't arranged to meet Phoebe in the woods. In fact, she was surprised to see me. We got lost. We came to a highway. Since we were cold and hungry, we decided to have breakfast. *I* felt like running away, but Phoebe said that was crazy."

He was very careful to put down the truth and nothing but the truth. It wasn't the *whole* truth, but he didn't feel as guilty as he probably should have (criminal instinct).

Instead of writing his personal statement (optional), he composed five poems, expressing for posterity how he felt at the time. The longest was two pages; the shortest, three lines.

> She holds an owl upon her knee,
> Who whoos a dreary melody.
> I wish that she was holding me.

He put his heart and soul into these poems (i.e., it was a symbolic owl), but at the last minute (thank God), he decided not to submit them. Probably no other human being would know what they were even supposed to be about, let alone mean.

His dad, when he called back, sounded calm like everybody else, though you could tell from his calmness that he was disappointed in his one and only son. He asked several practical questions—"just to understand the situation"— then said he'd be there on Thursday.

"You teach on Thursday."

"I'll cancel my classes."

"Don't. There's nothing you or anybody can do. If they kick me out, I have an open ticket for the shuttle that would just go to waste. I can get home all right." After a pause, he said, "I'm sorry, Dad."

It felt weird to have his two worlds come together like this, albeit briefly.

* * *

He didn't have to appear before the whole faculty, just the Disciplinary Committee, which met every Thursday at ten o'clock. He couldn't sleep the night before, not even for a few minutes. He kept rehearsing worst-possible scenarios. He remembered a story Boris had told him once. When he (Boris) was a young man, a samizdat pamphlet was circulated among Russian intellectuals, containing suggestions for how to evade the KGB's questions. For example, if the agent asked, "From whom did you get the gospel?"—because in those days it was dangerous to own a Bible—you were supposed to say, "From Matthew."

But that was a noble breaking of the law, like Thoreau's civil disobedience. Tim was guilty of being horny all the time: That was his real crime. Compared to hiding a Bible in Soviet Russia, it was pretty pathetic.

At around three o'clock, as if to punish himself, he tried pummeling Woody. At four o'clock he got out of bed and took one of the little white pills the infirmary prescribed for all ailments. He used spit so he didn't have to go down the hall to the drinking fountain. Instead of knocking him out, though, it made him jittery. His heart seemed to be beating in another part of the room—not in his chest where it belonged. Then it was morning, there was light against the shade, and someone was making a racket out in the hall. He had to get up whether he felt like it or not.

When he entered the Bunting Room at ten o'clock, all the birds mounted on the walls looked like former students that had gotten shot. The members of the committee stood up and shook his hand. There were seven of them, including Ms. Whimbrel, whose smile came and went. Snipe-Do was the chairperson.

His advisor, Mr. Grosbeak, went along to give him quote unquote moral support.

When the teachers all sat back down, Tim saw there was an empty chair at the table.

"Won't you join us, Tim?" Snipe-Do said almost cheerfully.

As soon as he sat down, they began asking him questions, which he tried to answer as honestly as he could. He remembers the questions better than his answers.

What exactly were you planning to do? Where would you have gone if Dean Grouse and Dean Swift hadn't found you? Tim, ah, why was Phoebe wearing your shirt and underwear? Do you honestly believe that you were acting responsibly toward her? What were you hoping to accomplish by running away? Do you feel like telling us about this fight you mentioned—between you and Phoebe? Well, then, has any other recent incident at school made you feel pressured?

Mr. Woodcock asked him to come up with an adjective that he felt described him.

"Alien from outer space?" Tim said, smiling.

" 'Alien,' at least in that sentence, is a noun," said the Boner.

"Oh yeah," said Tim, running his fingers through his hair. His cap was in his lap. "Alien being?"

Somebody else said, "What do you think would have happened if you had pulled something like this in Russia? What has your parents' reaction been? Do you feel you've let them down? How do you think you're going to feel about all this five years from now?"

Snipe-Do let everyone else ask their questions first, then she said, "Uh, Tim, do you remember last year when we read *The Odyssey* together?"

As soon as she said that, he realized he was a goner.

It was like he suddenly noticed how dark the large, cavernous room was. The only light seemed to be coming from the high windows, which adorned two of the walls and which you could only see gray clouds out of.

He just knew she was going to falsely accuse him of plagiarism again, but instead she said, "Do you remember the epithet most frequently used to describe Odysseus?"

" 'The great tactician,' " Tim said in a rusty voice. "Sometimes he was called 'wily.' "

"Exactly," Snipe-Do said, and then, apropos of nothing, she smiled at him. Taken by surprise, Tim couldn't help smiling back.

"And, as I recall, you pointed out once that Odysseus was Telemachus's role model. Does that mean you think these are positive qualities? Nowadays, I guess we'd say that Odysseus had 'political savvy,' that he 'knows how things work.' "

"Maybe," Tim said. The chair under his bottom felt hard. "What I said was, it all depended on what ends that wiliness was used for. I mean, if Odysseus was wily just to, like, get a lot of plunder, that would seem less noble."

He couldn't believe they were saying these words to each other. Nobody else could know what they were talking about, but he and Snipe-Do did.

"Yes, but if you remember," the English teacher said, "our hero was not averse to riches. And he was certainly not what you or I would call selfless. But he did use his wiliness in what I guess we'd both call a good cause: to help the people he loved."

Tim had to look away. He was grinning so hard his cheeks hurt.

Snipe-Do said softly, "You see, Tim, I remember what

you wrote in your *Odyssey* paper. In fact, I've sometimes thought I would like to read it again."

He quickly looked at her. "I don't have it anymore," he murmured.

"We're talking about a paper Timur wrote for me last year," she explained briefly to her colleagues. "At the time, I could hardly believe he had written it." Her eyes fastened on Tim. "I think I owe you an apology."

"It's okay."

"Now, Tim," she hurried on in her teacher's voice, "let's reason together." This phrase was kind of a joke in her class because she always said that when she was trying to get a discussion going. "It would be *very* easy for you to simply say that you had gotten up early to run the Daily Mile, too—which you and I know isn't true. But then the burden would be on us to somehow prove what is far more probable: that the two of you simply spent the night in the woods together."

Tim listened, interested.

"I assume that's what we're going to hear after lunch: 'I was trying to get my Mile in before classes started.' Since apparently we have to be legalistic about these things, *is* that why you were out of your dorm before six?"

"No," he said, giving his head a single shake.

"*Did* you go to the woods, hoping to run into Phoebe?"

"Yes," he said, nodding once.

"And she went there to meet you?"

"No," he said in a loud, clear voice. "Really. I'm telling the truth."

A shadow crossed Snipe-Do's face. "But *you* went to be with her—and *not* to run the Daily Mile?"

"Yes."

Snipe-Do looked at him. "Tim," she said, "you and I both know that you aren't exactly a dodo, so I guess I'm wondering why you seem so willing and eager to admit everything. Is it to protect Phoebe?"

He shook his head.

"Do you *want* us to fire you?"

That, by the way, is what they called it up there. You didn't get "expelled," you got fired.

He cleared his throat. "No. I don't want you to fire me."

"No," the sharp-eyed English teacher said, "but 'no' with a qualification? If you are required to leave, it won't be the end of the world?"

Tim shrugged.

"Maybe it would be helpful if you tried to tell us what you don't like about being here."

Good grief! he thought, his shirt and tie suddenly strangling him.

She sat there, waiting, the way she used to wait in English class—for two or three minutes, if necessary, until you quote unquote expressed yourself.

"I like it here," he said, hearing himself how lame that sounded. "But I miss my family. Boarding school still feels a little strange. To me. A little artificial. I like my dorm parents—they're nice to us." He glanced at Mrs. Whimbrel, sitting there, immaculately coiffed. "I don't know, it's just not the same as your own parents."

"What else?" Snipe-Do prompted, when he halted. "What do you really think of this school?"

He wouldn't have minded so much telling her in private. It was embarrassing to try and say this in front of a whole group of teachers. It was like insulting people to their faces.

"It's a very good school," he said. "Academically speaking. I like my classes. However, sometimes I feel I'm being trained not just intellectually, but also—like, I'm being taught certain values without being asked to stop and consider if I really value them. It's hard to put into words."

"For example?"

Why did she keep bugging him, bugging him? Maybe he should answer for a change—*tell her how he felt*—and let her see how she liked it.

"Sometimes," he said, in a voice growing louder, "it seems like I'm supposed to live up to some public image instead of just being who I am. Sometimes it's a struggle to remain Timur. I feel like I'm forgetting where I came from. I'm Russian and American—both. I want to go on feeling both, not just be the Russian kid who's trying to disguise himself as an American. Maybe it would be like this at any school, but AP has so much—I don't know the correct word: dominating personality—that after a while, just being here, you feel yourself—your *self*—disintegrating."

No one interrupted him, so he went on.

But it was also habit-forming, being at AP. The things he liked about it, he liked a lot. He knew they were on the fast track. He wanted to succeed—who didn't? But maybe everything was happening too fast for his own good.

"And Phoebe? How does she fit into what you're saying?"

"I love her."

"I'm sure you do, but what I mean is, do you think this is a good school for *her*?"

He smiled. "She likes being on the fast track. Maybe she belongs there."

In the privacy on his own mind he was thinking that AP *wasn't* a good place for her, but it wasn't his business to speak for her. Besides, where else could she go? To her dad's, her mom's?

Tim would have gladly made a home for her, if he could, but he was only sixteen.

Snipe-Do's voice interrupted his thoughts. "What if she's allowed to stay, and you're sent home?"

He pictured himself in his dad's car, speeding up the interstate. If he got sent home, it would be like getting off at the next exit and having to drive down back roads.

He said, "Late at night, I'm like, *what* am I doing? But the next morning I feel strong again."

"Thank you, Tim," Snipe-Do said softly. Then she added in her chairperson's voice, "Does anybody have a final question?"

"I do," Ms. Whimbrel said. "What have you learned from this experience, Timothy?"

He thought that was what he had been trying to explain, but they were all on the edges of their seats, so he blurted, "It's better to have loved and lost than never to have loved at all?"

But even though it's a famous saying, it can't have been the right answer. But at least everybody smiled and looked relieved. Without Tim's evidence there was no clear-cut case against Phoebe—or anyone else. That meant that the famous lawyer Phoebe's father had hired, who was biding his time at Webber's Pond Inn, could go home without filing a suit against the school.

Tim was sent out of the room. Half an hour later Mr. Grosbeak came out, too, and walked him to the dining hall. His advisor wasn't supposed to tell what was said behind closed doors, but he did anyway. Snipe-Do was the only one on Tim's side. If they punished him for being so candid, she said, what message would they be sending to the student body?

But somebody else pointed out that if they *didn't* punish him for flagrantly breaking the before-hours rule, what message would they be sending to the student body?

The vote was six to one in favor of expulsion.

"She really got wound up," his advisor told him. "She stood up and made a speech, saying that you had been dropped into a foreign environment and had made some errors in judgment, but that in the face of adversity you had maintained your integrity and stood by the person you loved. She said that this was a sad day for you, but an even sadder day for the school."

"Ms. Snipe-Dowitcher said all that?"

Tim had always thought she hated his guts.

A lot of kids came up to him in the dining hall and shook his hand, as if someone in his family had died. "It's okay," he kept saying. "Thanks."

Julie Crake and Freddy Goatsucker and a few other kids sat at the same table as him. Julie ate a small salad. She kept glaring at Phoebe, who had to sit at a separate table with her advisor, Ms. Killdeer. "If I ever had a boyfriend, I would never betray him," Julie stated softly in Tim's ear.

He looked at her. "You're a good friend, Julie. Will you write to me?"

His last night, he went and stood in front of the Rookery. In every lit window lived a kid whose name he at least knew. Music was coming from a forbidden stereo somewhere. The light from the Common Room spilled through the windows onto the bushes where he was lurking like one of the have-nots before the Russian Revolution (now everyone in Russia is a have-not).

He was supposed to just be getting his pajamas and toothbrush, because after you're kicked out of AP you have to spend your last night in the infirmary. That way you can't cause any more trouble. When you think about it, once they kick you out they don't have any more hold over you. You could break every rule in the book, if you wanted to. Unfortunately, he couldn't think of any other rules he felt like breaking.

When he had gotten everything he needed, Doc Whimbrel escorted him to the infirmary. On the way there Doc talked about how much the school had changed since the late fifties, when he was an Avian. "No loud stereos in those days. No drugs. *No girls.*"

I.e., the good old days.

"I feel for your generation," Doc said. "It's so much harder to be a boy nowadays, to know what's expected of you. I probably shouldn't be telling you this, but some of us aren't entirely persuaded that justice has been done."

It was the longest conversation he and his dorm father ever had in their lives. In the driveway to the infirmary, they shook hands. Then the good doctor said, "Move on," and started back to the dorm, probably to memorize some more verbs.

At first Tim thought he meant, Get a move on, i.e., NO STANDING. Then he realized he was just giving him more words to live by.

Incidentally, Phoebe's case came up, as scheduled, after lunch. She got probation, with a recommendation that she get counseling from the school shrink at least twice a month for the remainder of the school year. He would gladly pay $728.44 (which is how much he has saved so far to buy a car) to hear what she and Dr. Godwit talked about.

Ever
After

After he had been home for a couple of weeks, Tim lugged his father's old klunker of an IBM-PC up to his room one day. Boris had bought himself a new one, a Macintosh, but the IBM still worked. Out his window, through the black branches of their tree, Manhattan shone like a distant planet. His dad, who usually left him alone when he was up in his room, brought him a sandwich and a glass of milk.

Tim had tried to explain to his parents what had happened, but Aviary Prep was not a world they could understand. Now more than ever he felt his life belonged to him and him alone. All his parents could do was try and sympathize, based on what they knew. You told the truth, so it's okay. You didn't betray your friends. You didn't like the moral atmosphere, so you left—like the first pilgrims in their tall ships. Like the pioneers in their covered wagons. Like us, getting on the plane.

But he knew, without their saying so, that he had let them down—not by bringing home Bs instead of As, but by throwing into question the rightness of what they had done. Now he could probably forget about the American Dream—going to an Ivy League school.

"Why do you keep referring to yourself in third person?" Boris said, reading over his shoulder.

Timur just sat there patiently, waiting for him to leave. "I don't know. It makes it easier to tell the truth."

■

There isn't much more to tell.

Phoebe came over to Mr. Grosbeak's car, where Tim was

sitting on the passenger side, waiting to be driven to Logan Airport. She looked taller than usual, and sullen. Tim willed himself not to feel anything as she stuck an envelope through the half-opened window.

Chris Kite was waiting at the top of the stairs to Audubon Hall. When she had galloped up the stairs, he opened the door for her, but she stalked past, her head slightly bowed. Chris turned to grin at the Roosky in the car, then disappeared after her.

On the way to the airport Big Nose kept trying to think of famous Americans who had been kicked out of their boarding schools for one reason or another. Marlon Brando, John Cheever, Humphrey Bogart. There were some other names Tim didn't recognize.

" 'You have learnt something. That always feels at first as if you had lost something.' George Bernard Shaw," the English teacher added, when Tim just sat there.

Tim smiled at him, but he couldn't help wondering if Grosbeak liked him more for his mind or his butt. It's probably a homophobic thing to think, but he was in a rebellious mood.

It felt funny (not ha ha funny) to be driving to Boston on a school day. It felt mildly wrong—which is a *free* feeling.

"What if I don't get on the plane?" he said, raising his eyebrows.

For about two seconds Mr. Grosbeak looked worried.

"Just kidding."

"Maybe I should come with you to make sure you find your flight all right," the teacher stated nonchalantly, but at Logan he just got out and handed him his backpack. They shook hands. "Stay in touch."

He had to hurry back for his eleven o'clock.

*   *   *

The weather was pretty shitty—i.e., perfect, considering. He had to ride on five different means of transportion to get home. From La Guardia he took a bus that gave him a headache to midtown Manhattan, near Grand Central Station, and from there the Number Four train to the Staten Island Ferry.

He just missed the boat, so he went and used one of the terminal phones that smelled like a urinal to call home. His father's message was interrupted by his real father.

"It's me."

"Where are you? When are you coming home? Your mama is so upset. She is making everything you like. Pickled mushrooms. Cabbage soup. Roasted chicken with potatoes. Beet salad."

As soon as the ferry boat moved out through the giant portals of the terminal, the city became a blur in the background. Seagulls flew out of the fog and landed on the deck. They walked around and squawked a lot. The sound they make isn't that musical, but at least it makes you think of the sea.

Pretty soon all the other passengers went inside.

It had finally sunk in that he was going home. For ten and a half years home meant a big yellow building on Viktorenko Street, House Twelve, Apartment Eight. Not far from the Aeroport Station of the Moscow metro. You had to cross a busy street—he couldn't remember the name—then run up the unpaved alleyway that went along the back of the police academy. The alleyway was usually muddy—except in summer, when it was just dirt, or winter, when it was covered with snow. He could smell his mom's cooking as soon as he came through the front door. Where you first went in, there was this little room—*vestibule*—where you had to sit on the floor and pull off your boots. Then you put on your *tapochki* and went inside.

Then for almost a year they lived in a part of Queens called Jackson Heights—33-17 Eighty-Fourth Street, Apartment C-1—with cousin Yakov Truskinovsky, who had a splayed thumb, and his wife, Masha. That year was like a dream. Half the kids at his school spoke Spanish or Korean.

When his dad got a part-time job at Columbia, they moved to 301 West 108th Street, Apartment 9B, in Manhattan, right on the corner of Broadway, the most famous street in the world. You could see the Hudson River through the burglar gate. At night cockroaches partied in the kitchen because Boris was convinced that the stuff they used to kill them caused cancer. You could hear him shouting at the exterminators, No, you may not enter. By the way, go to hell. They lived there for just under three years, which is approximately how long it takes to become an American boy.

For a whole school year plus he lived in the Rookery Dormitory for Boys, at the prestigious Aviary Preparatory School, founded in 1801.

Now he was crossing New York Harbor, to their new house on Staten Island. In a few days he would no doubt be attending a public school in his own neighborhood. Maybe a girl there would find him fascinating, now that he had a past dot dot dot.

He took Phoebe's letter out of his back pocket. It was in an official envelope, Office of the Dean, which meant she had probably swiped it. Inside were two sheets of lined paper torn from a spiral notebook, sort of concave from being being sat on all day. The contents were pretty personal. At the end she enclosed the words to "their song," in case he had forgotten them.

> "'Tis the gift to be simple,
> 'Tis the gift to be free,
> 'Tis the gift to come down
> Where we ought to be;
> And when we find ourselves
> In the place just right
> 'T'will be in the valley
> Of love and delight.
> When true simplicity is gained
> To bow and to bend
> We shan't be a-sham'd
> To turn, turn will be our delight
> Till by turning, turning
> We come round right.

"Do you think we can ever be just friends? I wonder. I'm thinking of becoming a Shaker, because they take a vow of chastity and sometimes it seems like love is more complicated than it's worth (no offense)."

One second he was standing there, the letter flapping in the wind. The next he was bent over the railing, laughing hysterically. Ha, ha, ha, he laughed—in great gulping cries. He had nothing but the back of the envelope to wipe his eyes with.

When he looked up, Lady Liberty was standing in the mist, her green arm held high. The doors behind him were pulled open. Despite the biting wind, passengers flocked out onto the deck to take pictures. One man was talking into his camcorder. In Russia they say that when a camera clicks a bird flies out.

" 'To turn, turn,' " Tim started singing to the wind, " 'will be our delight. 'Till by turning, turning, we come round right.' "

He did a pirouette, then leaped like Misha Baryshnikov into the air. When nothing bad happened, he did it again. But, frankly speaking, it's hard to tell whether you've landed in the same place or not. He went and set his pack against the bulkhead (the rest of his stuff was being sent by UPS), then lined up the tips of his sneakers on a crack in the lineoleum. This time he made fists and worked his elbows up and down and jumped as high as was humanly—or rather, Timurly—possible. He landed with a thump more or less in the same place.

It was not what you could call a controlled experiment.

"Hey. You. Yeah, you." A man in an orange vest, one of the crew, was shouting at him. "Whatthefuck youthink youdoing?"

People were looking at him. He started to explain. He had to shout.

The man in the orange vest came hurrying up the metal stairs. "You'd come down in the same fucking place. Don't they teach you nothing in school nowadays?" He looked at Timur's face. "Whatsa madda wichew anyways?"

"Nothing. Watch once."

One of the tourists handed someone his camera and made some discreet jumps of his own, trying to watch himself and jump at the same time. His companion took his picture. Tim got off a good one this time. He went up, up, up, but he never learned the result because at the last minute, in preparation for docking, the boat swerved.